SEVEN NIGHTS

OF  *Love*

They encompass their entire lives within.......

P R PATEL

PARTRIDGE
A Penguin Random House Company

To order additional copies of this book, contact
Partridge India
000 800 10062 62
orders.india@partridgepublishing.com

www.partridgepublishing.com/india

To
My lovely wife
Monalisa

Few Persons in my life, without whom I would not be what I am today

- *My parents & family*
- *My friends and relatives*
  &
- *My special friends and well-wishers . . . my readers*

Thank you . . . thank you very much.

Present days:

$\mathcal{T}$hough last night was extremely sombre, today seems no unusual for Srijesh who returns in the same time of evening after giving his final lecture for this week. He can relax for the next two days and decides to have late dinner tonight. Five days of feverish work schedule made him to go for a long walk to the seashore. He believes it might alleviate his weariness, instead it offers him a deep thought of his past. Why today, he keeps on questioning him. But the truth is, it has actually commenced hunting him way beyond his capability of resistance from last few days. If average lifespan of human is considered sixty years, he has already crossed half of his journey five years ago. He is not a coward to ask himself every day, what he has received from life. For most of the individual's dictionary, the meaning of life might be a summation of happiness, adventure, love and friendship. But that doesn't mean it is a life of failure if someone has missed these achievements. He doesn't agree. Hundreds of people find solace, if they have only their basic necessities. So does Srijesh who is blessed with much more than just survival. Still he is living a plunder's life because of his lost past. And then . . . this night comes.

He finishes his dinner and his maid anxiously tells, "Anna, I have kept your letter and ticket on the table."

"Letter." Srijesh has completely forgotten about it.

"Yes, I have kept it on your table."

"Whether Amma slept?"

"Yes. Already."

"Ok, you also carry on."

"Bye, I will not come this weekend. Even you are also travelling."

Srijesh has not been able to make up his mind for this journey. He goes to the terrace taking a glass of scotch in hand. Gentle breeze is providing fantastic companion with every sip of scotch along with the moonlight and the distant visual of seacoast. Mahe, Puducherry, a union territory

1

located in coastal part near Kerala is his native; he lives here with his mother and a maid who supports them in their day today activities.

He continues drinking; however one glassful of scotch couldn't retard him from acknowledging his past and he needs some more to have a stress free sleep. He then goes inside to pour another glass but inadvertently draws a flash to his bedroom, where the invitation letter is lying hopeless. Bonded in a red envelop, it is a letter from a very own friend. And he has thrown it in some corner of his house bearing a little amount of jealousy. From a very long time he has not received this kind of letters. He again feels tempted to open it. His hands tremble surrounded with some unknown sensation and whenever he tries to read it, he feels completely evaporated from his state of intoxication. He never knows this invitation card will change his life and invite him again to his very own place, he considered till date.

"GOA"

But this one is not exactly the invitation which wrote his fate. It was a letter he had received many years back. It was an invitation for Christmas. And that time, he was just twenty two years of old and had finished his Masters.

1

"*I*t is Suju Uncle's," Hena, Srijesh's little sister told loudly after receiving the letter from Postman.

DEAR SRIJESH, IT IS HIGH FEVER. DOCTOR TOLD. I AM IN BED. WAITIN FOR YOU COME AND ADMIT ME. YOUR UNCLE SUJU.

From writing itself it is evident that Suju has sent this letter. It is his trademark style. Capital bold which he knows, but one thing he doesn't. It contains every time a heavy load of ridiculous spelling mistakes. Srijesh smiled as he knows it is a blunder from Suju and he applies this kind of weapon whenever he feels to invite him. But this letter strikes the perfect chord leaving everybody terrified in the family.

"What time is the train?" Srijesh's father asked.

"Let me prepare some food. I will parcel some Ayurveda medicine also for Suju," Srijesh's mother told binding some motherly sentiments in her voice.

"Amma, don't bother. I don't want anything."

"Not for you, poor boy is alone there having fever. At least take something for him."

Srijesh felt pity by looking at this scenario just because of Suju's meaningless letter. But he must thank Suju, as his throwaway sheet of paper enables him to go to his place again, which they both have planned one day, to celebrate Christmas in Goa where Suju stays.

Half of the day goes in discussing about Suju and his bad health, as if no topics are left in the house. But when the day started running, everyone was concerned that Srijesh will be

3

leaving after sometime. And finally it was decided, Srijesh has to catch the night train today.

It was drizzling in Mahe that day. Though Srijesh is exalted to go to Goa, but is every time painful for him to leave the home. He took bathe in the pond situated backside of his house and plucked two Lilies without any reasons. By the time he came back home, few dishes were already cooked. Mother was in a damn hurry in preparing as much food as possible in limited amount of time. Looking at Srijesh, his sister wanted to tease him for a while and targeted the Lily flowers.

"Maybe you forgot to give the Lilies to somebody."

"Huh! You can give it to your boyfriend if you like."

"Ohh . . . giving me a consolation as you are leaving today. Go and have food. Your favourite dish is prepared."

"Really. Come, we will have it together."

"Aha . . . I am not blessed like you. Our loving son."

And she got stared by Srijesh.

"Hena, what are you doing amma, please help me in preparing," Mother called her from kitchen.

"Coming . . ." And she left by showing a twisted mouth.

Even before the leaving time comes, Srijesh's mind has slowly shifted from the lush greenery of Mahe to the sunny beaches of Goa. Emotions started swapping from his mother land to the place he loves next. He has been staying in Goa for last two years and completed his masters there. He is mad about every bite of Goa and the sand, water, paddy fields, coconut grooves are the causes of his temptation so far. The place has taught him many things and he misses his guitar and music. He never feels away from his home. And this belongingness has successfully occupied him for last two years in Goa. He feels they are calling him up. God, how can he control the excitement? He tells himself, "Steady, steady." But why is it increasing so sturdy this time? Is destiny pulling him for a new adventure? Only time can tell.

He was accompanied by his father to the station.

"Appa, don't wait. Chance of rain. Please carry on. Mother will be worried."

"I wish you would have stayed for the Christmas."

His father asked for which he was not having any answer. He smiled and touched his feet. An indirect symbol to say goodbye to the senior.

"Ok, just take care of Suju." The words came from the softest corner of his father's heart. It is he, once who asked his younger brother Suju to leave Mahe and get a job somewhere. He repents all the time for what he has said and done. As the eldest in family, he never dares to show his weakness. But Suju was also an intolerable boy when he was in Mahe.

Father left after putting a five hundred rupee note in Srijesh's pocket. He knew, Srijesh's friends have come to see him off and he didn't want to be an obstacle. Within seconds friends gathered and started hounding him.

"This time at least ten bottles. What are your plans this new year, when you will be back . . . blah . . . blah?" Nobody could hear anything properly. With endless communication, final bell rang and Srijesh left after saying a good bye to his friends.

Night was sleeping with a rhythmic sound and Srijesh looked out of the window. It was full moon dancing above the black clouds. With a song in mind and a whispering tune in mouth, Srijesh slept till the night accompanied him. Good night Mahe. See you soon.

2

KOLKATA, WEST BENGAL.
DURING THE SAME TIME.

*I*t was 11 o' clock night in the ladies hostel and girls were going to sleep.

"Ok, good night."

"How you can dear, whereas your friend has almost lost her sleep," Sibangini told Ritee after throwing a pillow on her face.

"Hey, what is your problem?"

Sibangini suddenly jumped into Ritee's bed and pushed her butt a little.

"Don't be mean. You are my friend."

"That's why I am telling you to sleep," Ritee suggested Sibangini.

"How can I? How can I?"

In-between a snoring Chandrima asked her friends, "Oh please, at least let me sleep, you two."

"Shhhhh."

"Is she more beautiful than me?" Sibangini asked.

"Who?"

"Arey, Prof. Ignesh's would be wife."

"Okay, so that is the problem." Ritee realized the condition of Sibangini. She has a one-sided crush on Prof. Ignesh who is getting married in a week's time. And that is why Sibangini has turned into amnesia.

"There is no doubt about that," Swati chucked a mocking comment at Sibangini from the other corner of the room.

"Shut up."

"Anyways, you people are going for the marriage. You can see her and decide," Ritee said.

"What do you mean by you people . . . . ? We people." Sibangini gave a surprised look at Ritee.

"Hey, seriously. I am not interested to go at all."

"You are saying no to Goa. To Goa. Arey, we will not get second time chance my dear," an anxious Sibangini pushed her words further.

"What is special in Goa? Our Kolkata is best," Ritee gave a chauvinistic reply.

"But at least for a change."

"I don't need a change," Ritee firmed her stance once again.

"You know your problem. You are not in love. May be you will find your true love in Goa."

"Hah, what a joke. For searching a true love I don't need to go Goa. I am happy here and will get a nice guy in my lovely place on earth Kolkata."

"At least let's go and attend the marriage. I have not seen a Christian family marriage. And above all, Professor has invited all of us with lots of expectations. We must oblige."

"Don't make us fool Sibangini. You are excited only because you can see the bride and evaluate whether to be jealous or not. Am I right?" Swati started examining Sibangini's impatience.

"Jealous. My foot. She will be a waste. Professor will repent for his entire life and will never get satisfied, neither mentally or physically."

Poor Professor. He must be preparing himself for his first honeymoon and girls have already predicted his incompetent sex life. Ignesh Fernandes used to be a talented scholar of his time and hence became the youngest Professor in college. He is the most lovable person in college and girls are diehard fan of him. He likes his students very much and students also love him too. That is why; he has invited most of his favourite students to visit his native Goa and to attend his marriage.

Girls are too smart. Nobody's parents would have given a clean chit for the journey until they rename it as a 'study tour'. Yes. But even though for a study tour they need some fool breed on earth to post them safely to Goa. And the scapegoats became few college mates. Those were Parthoda, Chaterjee and Banku.

Girls started bickering and were still undecided for the tour. And finally Ritee nodded for the risk free journey as senior people like Parthoda and Banku were joining them. Typical girl character. She has already dreamt about the holiday but reluctant to express it. And that particular time who knows that it is going to change Ritee's life forever. Once she was unwilling to join has now become the most active participant of the team. But she still doddles for the entire night, what stupid Sibangini told her. Does she have to travel a long way to Goa to find her love, what rubbish?

She does not know; there exists a superior magnetic force which was pulling her down to Goa.

Where in one part of the country there was celebration to go for the adventure, in other part it was like a home coming.

3

GOA.
DURING THE BEAUTEOUS WINTER.

*I*t was a chilled morning in Goa as it rained last night. It was cold and breezy when Srijesh stepped out of Margaon Station. Rubbing his palms he asked for a cup of tea in nearby shop. He was expecting Suju to come till he finishes his tea. They have been celebrating Christmas for the last two seasons in Goa and keeping his promise, Srijesh has come back in the right time. But unfortunately the same was not visible by Suju who forgot to receive him in station. Almost half an hour passed in the tea shop but there was no sign of Suju's arrival

The moment he pulled a five rupee note to pay for the tea, he knew he is not going to get back the change.

"Sorry sir. No change." The reply came as expected.

Suju didn't come, three rupees change gone and he is not having strength to have one more cup of tea neither to wait for Suju.

And suddenly, one horrible tribal look boy called him from the opposite side of the road.

"Bhaiya, oh . . . Srijesh Bhaiya. Come this side, oh . . . hello, this way."

Srijesh slowly approached and recognized him. It is Chotu. He is a boy from Jharkhand, over matured from his age and has come to Goa last year. He used to work for a Mangalore based coconut farm owner. A boy of 5ft tall and a body weight of 30kg, Chotu was picked by his master only because he defeated him in climbing coconut tree. His present age won't be more than fourteen but he is blessed with immense strength of agility. If child labour had been strictly followed, this fellow would have been a genuine case by then.

"How are you Chotu?"

"You brought food."

"Idiot. You didn't bother to ask me how I am and how my journey was, straight asking about food. Anyways, throw your worries somewhere, I have brought enough," Srijesh consoled him even though he knows, it will not be sufficient for Chotu who can have six times meals per day. Chotu's 30 kg body can easily engulf 10kg of food. One more blessing from God.

"Where is Suju Uncle by the way?" Srijesh asked.

In reply, Chotu gave a crooked smile with a shrewd answer, "You will come to know about Guru once you reach house."

"Guru." This is what Chotu pronounces him. Now a middle aged bachelor Suju was once an unwanted child in his native and knowing his potential of not able to clear his secondary exam, he escaped and fled from Mahe. He came to Goa some twenty years back in search of the basic necessities of life. But his loyalty in work paid the royalty for him and now he is one of the most wanted people in Goa apart from being a budget hotel supervisor. He is a one stop solution for all the requirements imposed by the tourists in South Goa. And he performs his duty with utmost sincerity. He is adorable and gifted with a great sense of humour which attracts female tourists the most. But no man is perfect, so does Suju. He is an incorrigible flirt and his philander attitude has served some best social services to the women who are in search of hidden pleasure. Apart from mastering the art of sex, he is also a specialist in communicating some widely famous languages. He can speak most of the European languages with ease along with English and Hindi. But there is one more problem, the way he has articulated the command over good languages, he has got an equal fluency in bad languages too. And that is why he is called as Guru by his disciple Chotu and whatever slang Chotu knows, it is a gift from him. Chotu praises his Guru, being an ardent follower and he blindly follows his footsteps always. From last few months when chotu became jobless, it is his Guru who recommended a job for him in the same hotel and he is now staying with Suju and Srijesh in their house like a family member to them.

Before the sunshine gets unbearable, Srijesh and Chotu reached their house, their own place, very near to the beautiful Kolva Beach.

Slowly and silently the dark cloud passed away when the sun started smiling. Srijesh loves this part the most. He misses this sunshine and this beautiful beach for a long period of time.

"Don't finish the food till I come back."

By telling it so, Srijesh took his shirt off and ran incessantly into the sea water. He could see the sun kissing the radiant water and the seashore getting blushed by the romantic response of the rays. He could feel the sand sliding under his naked feet. His thrust became active when he threw the glossy bubbles into the air and dived into the sea.

"Have you gone mad?" Chotu called him loudly.

"Yes, yes, yes. Take as much food as possible. I don't want anything," Srijesh's excitement spoke for him. He is so obsessed for the charm of this place that every time he jumps into the seawater makes him feel of relieving all the strain of his mind. It feels divine to him always. One hour of sea bath turned his eyes into complete red, his body trembled but relaxed while he came back inside the house. Wiping his head in a towel he casually asked Chotu, "Some foods are still left. You have become a changed man Chotu. Whether food is not good?"

"No Bhaiya. It is very tasty. But If Guru comes to know, that I finished it alone, then he will bang my butt."

And then suddenly someone banged the door outside. Think of the devil and the devil has come.

A big, "HELLOOOOOOO."

"Darling, Sweetheart, you came." Suju entered the house like enemies enter the Queen's palace during night. He embraced Srijesh followed by some breathless kisses and welcomed him with his idiotic style of welcoming.

"Stop, stop it." Srijesh was unable to speak and half able to breathe, "What is this Uncle?"

11

"Hey, sorry, sorry. I can't control my excitement after seeing you. You know that." And as usual Suju was in his histrionic self.

"Oh stop it. By the way, where have you been?"

"Nowhere, I was just sleeping . . . ."

Chotu raised his eyebrows as he was expecting a shocking truth from Suju.

"What? I just slept in hotel. And you fucker, don't stare at me like that. Anyways, Srijesh you tell. How are you and how is Hena, your mother, back in family?"

"They are fine . . . including father."

"Just answer me what I asked, did I sound asking about your father, did I?"

Srijesh smiled and gave a witty expression to Suju. "Okay, Okay. Come, let's have food. Mother has sent for you especially."

"I know it. She never forgets me, unlike your father."

Srijesh served the balance food items. Suju took one bite and fed Srijesh.

"I was missing you very much and I LOVE YOU," Suju told aloud. Though Suju is his uncle in blood relation, but he shares the relationship of a brother and a friend at the same point of time with Srijesh. He loves him so much and can do anything for his nephew.

By realizing they can't finish the food without the kind cooperation from Chotu, they invited him for his second innings breakfast. And when Chotu joined them, the food disappeared at the rate of steam.

"Okay Srijesh, you take rest. We will bring some non-veg items and drinks for today evening. Let's go Chotu."

"No need uncle, it's ok."

"Arey, how can it be man? After so many days you have come here. At least we deserve one party tonight. Isn't it Chotu?"

"Yes Boss." And Chotu got elated as he is going to get some fabulous drinks tonight. His Srijesh Bhaiya has come and Suju will not offer him the cheaper drinks what he used to buy most of the time.

Srijesh knows, Suju is not bringing the drinks only to cheer his arrival, but he will tell his numbers of short time love stories, rather porn stories while getting boozed. Suju and Chotu left for the market as their conversation slowly became unheard. It was noon and Srijesh was so sure that if he closes his eyes now, he is not going to get up till evening. But the tiredness of his body shut his eyes and he went for a deep sleep. He could have slept for some more time if the mutton gravy smell would not have tilted him to wake up. He came out of the balcony by slowly rubbing his eyes and saw the beautiful sight of the house decorated with mini light bulb, which is a normal tradition in Goan family during Christmas. Some people have the craze of celebration and decorate and others follow the custom.

Suju used to be an excellent cook and he has almost finished preparing the side dish of mutton gravy and rice. The main dish was none other than everybody's favourite whisky and beer. But this sounds incomplete in absence of some chicken starter, which Chotu was preparing with plenty of concentration by creating the campfire where chicken was being grilled in the skewer. It was evening in Kolva Beach and the polished moonshine started falling on the seashore as an alternate source of light other than campfire. Srijesh realized no evening would be better than this one.

"Okay, okay guys. Be ready, there are two surprises for Srijesh." Suju came near to the campfire and started announcing after handing over each one a beer bottle.

"Cheers to Srijesh's home coming."

"Uncle, you were telling something." Srijesh tried to remind anxiously.

"Oh, yes. The first one is . . . Ms. Parker has agreed to send her two sons to learn guitar from Srijesh. And more over, she will pay thousand rupees per month."

"Wow. Really, But how come you convinced them Uncle. Her husband seems to be very rude and not much interested in music."

"What that poor fellow will do, he is just like a pet dog of their family. All decisions are taken by Ms. Parker herself.

And her husband is a shit," Suju told as if he is the personal secretary of Ms. Parker.

"But still Uncle, how could you manage to convince them?"

"There is only one way to convince and Guru did the same. He slept with her," said Chotu after gaining maximum energy from boozing.

"Bastard, I will kill you. She is my master. These fucking drinks you are having now are from her money, you don't know," Suju blasted with a tensed voice but Chotu hardly gets intimidated knowing it is normally the beer & whisky boil on behalf of Suju.

"Easy, easy Uncle."

And Suju gave a crooked smile for a tipoff.

"Is it? Really? Wuh . . . ho . . . what are you saying?" Chotu and Srijesh could not believe Suju.

"But how did you persuade her, she must be damn beautiful and you are no better than coalmine."

"What nonsense. You people are praising me or . . . ?"

"Ok, no offence, please continue." They requested as they can't afford a pause in the story.

"Fine, so the truth is . . . I slept with . . . with . . ." Suju was not able to complete the sentence, while Srijesh and Chotu were voraciously waiting for the truth to be exposed.

"One, two, and three . . . I slept with her mother."

"What? Ahh . . ." Srijesh and Chotu were about to vomit. Both of their eyes turned fire in surprise, which blinked for numerous times and they looked nauseated.

"Uncle, how could you? Ms. Parker will be no less than forty and her mother will be touching sixty."

"Hey, that's rubbish. She got married quite early man." Suju tried to defend his holy act performed with his so called girlfriend.

"Yeah, must be a child marriage, isn't it Guru?" Chotu replied naively.

"Oh just shut up stupid. She is just fifty five," Suju defended as if fifty five years is considered as a tender age for him.

"Ohh . . . just fifty five. And you slept with her."

In reply, Suju twinkled in front of Srijesh and shook his head which implied a strong yes.

"But Guru, how this indigestible thing happened by the way?" Chotu asked by forming a curiosity in mind.

"It is all thanks to my favourite local Feni drinks man. After a long drive old lady asked me, do you have something to drink?" Suju did mimicry of Italian accent, "and I took one glass of Feni and mixed some local stuff. Old lady got instant recharge man."

"And then you dig into her," Srijesh asked.

"No, she dug into me, ha ha," Suju replied by offering a clap to Chotu and Chotu followed him in laughing.

"Oh shit, Uncle how could you?"

"Arey, don't worry man, this was not the first time. You know, my first experience was also like this. She was more than double of my age when I was only eighteen. But what an experience, what an experience? It was killer man killer." Suju explained as if he saw heaven that time, "I am telling you both, when you go for the first time, search for a senior mate. It is equally good as opting for an old wine for a great taste," Suju said.

Chotu tried to touch his Guru's feet for this incredible achievement but his head tossed the whisky bottle and it fell down for a second.

"Arey, watch it man." And suddenly Suju saved the disaster when he caught the bottle. "Thank God, It was about to be empty, make one more glass for all." Suju and Srijesh took one more piece of grill chicken and all three raised the toast once again.

"Guru, you are successful for numbers of times. But I am not even one time lucky; don't you feel pity for your student, don't you?" Chotu asked by filling all the politeness and diplomacy in his question.

"Hey, why you are telling a lie man? Shall I open your secret?"

"Which one?"

"Beating in the bush."

"No, no, please," Chotu begged and put the index finger on his own lips which he later realized, should have been put on Suju's mouth.

"Uncle, which one?" Now Srijesh is eager to know.

And Suju disclosed it amidst a number of objections from Chotu after finishing one more peg.

"You know Mangalorean."

"Mangalorean, his ex-master right. Yeah, then."

"His daughter is his girlfriend."

"Seriously."

"No, no, not at all," Chotu blushed.

"You shut up." Suju became stubborn.

"Really, but he has got three daughters, which one?" Srijesh asked.

"Arey, the younger one . . . the 7th standard girl . . . arey that fat, buffalo look girl . . ." Suju tried to remind him from every possible angle but Srijesh could not make out and then suddenly Chotu jumped into this conversation and said, "Arey Bhaiya, the girl with biggest boobs among the three sisters."

Srijesh and Suju took a sharp turn towards Chotu and looked at him shockingly.

"What?"

"Bugger, she is not your girlfriend huh and you have already measured her body parts." Both kicked Chotu resulted the whisky bottle completely fell down to the ground.

"Oh my God, whether something left?"

Chotu bent the bottle to one eighty degree and concluded, "It is gone." They finished the whisky bottle and now the time was to grab the last bottle of Feni which gave them the strongest kick among all.

"You know Srijesh, what exactly happened? I was walking through the seashore off the coconut grove behind Mangalorean's house that evening. In a trice, I felt the bushes were shaken loudly. I thought why it is so man as there was no wind at all. I thought it might be a platoon of dogs, and then . . ." Suju resumed laughing without completing his story.

"Arey, tell Uncle, then what happened?"

"Oh my God, Chotu you tell man." Suju started crawling with big laughter on his face and was not able to produce any voice. And Srijesh too smiled along with Suju.

"Why you guys are laughing. Nothing happened," Chotu replied innocently again.

"What nothing happened, I saw both of you. I could clearly recognize you both," Suju affirmed.

"What will happen? The moment I removed my underwear, she ran away like a Mother Buffalo."

"What."

"That means nothing happened. Really. Arey bugger, you removed your underwear first, instead you should have done the contrary."

They both teased Chotu for the entire night. Gradually when Feni was about to finish, Chotu brought rice and mutton curry, but they have already had their main course of dinner. Their favourite whiskey. In the entire conversation nobody realized that the second surprise was actually remained untold. But they hardly bothered as it was one of the funniest nights they spent after a long time.

One can certainly expect a lazy morning after this kind of rendezvous during the night. Srijesh wanted to sleep some more time but affected by the intense snoring of Chotu. It is Sunday and Chotu gets a day off from his work. Srijesh got up slowly and approached towards the wash basin at the corner most place of the house. Finally a letter was kept on the dining table addressed to Srijesh, where it was written:

SORRY DUD, I FORGET YESTERDAY SUREPRISE TO GIVE. JUST TURN YOUR ASS AND SEE ONE BIG BLACK . . . BAG . . . IT IS NOT FROM ME. FROM MS. PARKER, BUT I MADE HER TO GIVE. OPEN IT AND ENJOY.

In a hurry the writer has forgotten to mention his name. But Srijesh knows, nobody dares to write this kind of letter other than Suju. The patented style. Capital bold and silly spelling mistakes. Curiosity revolved around him as he wanted to know what he gets if he turns his ass. And he

17

found exactly what was written in the letter. A BIG BLACK BAG but contains a marvellous gift inside. A guitar. Suju knows his passion for music. Once Srijesh has told, he will teach free of cost if somebody presents him a guitar. But more over he is going to get fees also.

"Love you Suju Uncle. You are truly a darling."

He started playing the guitar with its maximum volume causing Chotu to wake up furiously as if somebody struck an electric shock in his balls. But without damn bothering, Srijesh composed different tunes one after another. For the entire day he kept himself engaged in playing guitar apart from having food in some regular intervals. And Chotu, like a geek observer gave him company having no choice left. But inwardly, he wanted to bang the guitar into molecules which completely screwed his Sunday morning sleep.

4

The joy augmented to further leap among the girls, when Parthoda the mentor of the journey handed over the train tickets to them. Along with their baggage all were carrying their own expectations, in search of some lovely memories and blissful charm to Goa. But amongst all Sibangini was more excited, who was hardly bothered to see the new place but highly concerned to see the face of the bride. And the sense of animosity made her to pack excess of luggage which will empower her to wear best of the best dresses to overshadow others. Ritee and other girls smartly packed a few as per their requirements but literally got upset by seeing the extensive wardrobe of Sibangini. And it was Ritee who dared to ask her. "How many dresses are you taking?"

In reply, Sibangini posted an unnoticed reaction and started counting the packed clothes as per the numbers of days going to be spent. She kept on mumbling, "Thursday morning the red one, Friday the yellow one, for wedding the pink sari . . ." and still counting which obviously turned others at the heap of irritations.

"This is too much."

But Sibangini as expected untouched by their concerns and suddenly spoke out unconscious, "Hey girls, anybody got extra napkins. Journey time and you never know."

"Do you think we are fools?" Ritee gave a stared eyes look and went to the wash room.

"What happened to her? What I said?" an innocent Sibangini asked pointing at Ritee.

"She is already in her second day of period," Swati replied.

"Oh . . . so sad. How she will manage. It turns even worse in journey time. No?"

They all clenched their smile while Ritee entered the room and Sibangini resumed setting her wardrobe proving once again as the most anxious member among all.

They slept bit late that night after packing their bags with all the required things, their dresses, daily stuffs, and not to forget the napkins. Apart from that they all took their Bengali traditional saris in a planning to wear the same in the wedding date. May be for others it was to obey their tradition, but for Sibangini it would be the last chance to attract Prof. Ignesh.

Hardly slept for three to four hours, Ritee woke up to the foggy morning of winter. She can clearly observe the mist of fog filling the gap of the hostel window. Kolkata used to be very cool during December but the excitement of the journey was providing them enough warmth to prevail it. Except Ritee, everybody was enjoying the sound sleep of winter till the long needle touched the topmost part of the clock and gave an ugly sound of alarm.

"Hey Chandrima, Swati, Sibangini, wake up," Ritee shouted.

Girls took their own sweet time but surprisingly got ready prior to the expected time. They moved out of the hostel room along with three normal size air bags and one gigantic suitcase of Sibangini. They walked past the main gate and approached towards the meeting room outside the hostel compound where Parthoda, Chaterjee and Banku were waiting for them. It is Christmas vacation time and most of the students go to their natives, resulting meeting room looks empty which is normally occupied by the lovers to wait for their girlfriends.

"Hi girls, all set," Parthoda greeted like a Marshal greeting his army.

All respect Parthoda who is a final year LLB student and a closest relative of Chandrima. And Sibangini likes him because of his overgenerous attitude. One can travel entire country with Parthoda even if with empty pocket. He belongs to one of the richest families of Kolkata and has funded the entire cost of their trip. Irrespective of all, he is known for his selfless support to others.

When everyone assembled in one place, Chaterjee and Banku called for a taxi to proceed towards the busiest Howrah Railway Station. Train left as per the scheduled time. It was touching the time of afternoon still it was cold inside the train. Girls have slept for insufficient hours last night and feeling little tired leading to a low rate of gossiping. Else once Sibangini starts, it doesn't take much time to convert it to a fish market. They managed themselves properly inside the train and now one full compartment belongs to the troop. Among the guys, Chaterjee was more concerned towards girl's convenience, especially Swati who used to be his girlfriend and they were soon to become lovers by the help of Mediator Sibangini. Ritee could clearly make out and kept herself aloof by occupying her preferred distant window seat. They played cards till late evening, keeping the dinner parcel aside. Chaterjee was trying his best to lose the game against Swati to win her heart ultimately. He performed some magic tricks in cards whatever he has learnt from his hostel mates and was applying all his efforts to impress Swati. And silently his love flight was taking off inside the train. Unsure about the adventure this journey can offer them which only time could tell, they had their dinner as a matter of formality. Train started moderately but took the momentum during night. It crossed the border of West Bengal and was passing somewhere between the silent valley of costal Orissa. There was hardly any noise other than wind. The temperature level was falling sharply and inviting everybody for an irenic sleep.

Next day morning train has partially entered the southern part of the country and one can clearly predict by seeing the availability of breakfast. Outside food looks attractive always, but this time it tasted great too. Even to the appetite of Ritee who unanimously considers Bengali food as the best. The climate started altering as the new places were coming one after another, whose names were tough to pronounce and impossible to remind. They all had almost wiped the busy streets of Kolkata from their mind and started loving every pulse of the new places. The cold climate from yesterday took a sharp turn to warmer and gradually felt soothing. Sometimes the journey is memorable than the destination. And it happened exactly the same way for Ritee who was scared as her notion might get changed and reformed into a surprise truth. She could not sleep in the late evening unlike others and sat near to the window for a long while. She could feel the gentle breeze passing through the ears causing a strand of her hair misaligned. This time it was complete loneliness and Ritee didn't want to miss a sight. Fighting with the blow of wind, her eyelid wanted to extend a complete visual of outer world to the eyes. She could not undo her mascara getting spread over her blue eyes due to shedding a light drop of tear. Perhaps she was unsure whether the tear in her eyes is due to wind or something else. She kept on asking her if she has taken a right decision to come for the journey without informing her family. During late night Sibangini got a blink of Ritee and came to talk to her.

"Hey, I am observing the suffocation in you from yesterday. What happened dear, are you alright?"

Both realized they have hardly spoken to each other from the start of this journey. Like bosom friends they love to share their respective grieves to each other more than their happiness. Even having a reclusive characteristic, Ritee never hides anything to Sibangini and Sibangini treats her like own sister.

"Hey, are you alright?" Sibangini repeated her ask.

"Don't know, I am feeling guilty from inside. This is the first time I am going somewhere without informing my family."

"Don't worry; you are not alone who behaved like this. Nobody has told the truth to their parents. It is just a matter of seven days, everything will be fine."

"I am hoping so. I am praying, my father should not come to know," Ritee said quietly.

"Look dear. I suggest you to forget everything. You are going to a new place. Don't spoil your mood. Think to live full for the next seven days at least. I am sure you won't regret . . . unlike me. I am going to see him for the last time. At least the way I have seen him till now," Sibangini poised to her words and advised Ritee.

"You are hurt. Don't you?"

"Yeah I am. It is very difficult to forget the first love," Sibangini replied with tearful eyes.

Ritee realized she should console Sibangini, however till now it is happening the other way round.

"Only brave person can. And you are a brave girl dear." Ritee caused a smile on Sibangini's face. In return, she pulled Ritee's hand and folded with her palms.

"Let's pledge. Next seven days we are going to enjoy up to the fullest. No tear no sorrow."

Ritee Smiled.

"Arey, let's do it."

"Okay, I solemnly pledge."

The intensity of conversation vibrated Chandrima who asked subconsciously the most obvious question during the journey hours.

"Which station is it?"

"No idea, just sleep. We will reach tomorrow morning".

5

$\mathcal{I}$t has been two sleepless nights in Suju's mansion from the day Srijesh and Chotu came to know of having a task ahead to guide some Bengali tourists for the next seven days in Goa. Now the hot topics of discussion during the drinks hour are more about the Bengali girls than sex. Suju used to be the busiest person during Christmas, which made him to delegate the assignment to Chotu and Srijesh of escorting the Bengali tourists who were going to stay in Parker's Hotel.

"Hey boys, I hope you have not forgotten. And I don't want any complaint. Remember, they are referred by a VIP marriage function in Goa. Tomorrow morning train will arrive at 6.30. Be on time." Suju reminded the responsibilities of Chotu and Srijesh and went to sleep thereafter.

"Don't worry Guru. I will take care properly. They belong to nearby place from my native." Chotu's assertive answer led Suju for a tension free sleep that night. However he has almost spoilt Srijesh's mind, by an exaggeration of talk regarding Bengali girls and their beauties, from yesterday.

"Bhaiya, till date I have not seen attractive girls like Bengalis."

"Enough man, I think you are trying to overhype," Srijesh said.

"Bhaiya, you don't believe me right. You will realize once you see them. Perfect figure, fair colour and pure beauty. And if you see them in their Bengali sari, mark my words, you will squirt," Chotu replied by gently closing his eyes as if a sharp knife jabbed his sensation.

"Where have you experienced bugger?"

"In my village."

"In your village. You told your village is in Jharkhand."

"Of course. But there were some Bengalis migrated to our village. You made me remember our very own Dutta Family and his gorgeous wife. Half of our villagers had

24

a crush on her including few old men too. When she was going to take bathe in our village pond, everybody follows there. And it was making our day super fresh, if blessed to see her one unclothed body part at least. Seriously. It is highly impossible to control your fantasy if you see her. She is damn hot Bhaiya. B..E..A..U..T..I..F..U..L." Chotu projected the topic in such a way that it literally took Srijesh's mind to a fanciful world.

"And Bhaiya, one more secret. Bengali girls are lover of music. You have to show your calibre and they will chase you for sure. They love Bengali as well as Hindi music."

"Hindi. I can't even speak it properly." Srijesh showed his frustration of inability.

"Ha ha. Bhaiya, you are in blue moon from now on, huh." Chotu's naughty reply turned Srijesh blushed.

"Arey, stop it man. I am not. Anyways, you know how to speak Bengali?"

"No Bhaiya. But I can understand," Chotu replied.

"That's fine. Listen to me carefully. When we meet them, don't let them know you can understand Bengali. Ok."

"But why?"

"Don't be a fool man. If they come to know, they won't be revealing their personal gossip in front of us. There won't be any fun at all, do you realize that?"

Chotu thought for a while and concluded, "Bhaiya, you deserve a salute. I was thinking you are an innocent guy. But you are a great fucker than Guru." They carried on laughing and ran their hot topic for few more minutes before Chotu slept. Though Srijesh kept his eyes closed but could not sleep for long hours. Chotu's conversation has definitely portrayed a great excitement for tomorrow. Without presuming anything he felt intuitive for some memorable days to come this season.

6

$\mathcal{S}$econd part of the month of December is the best among the bests in this paradise. If the nights are beautiful in Goa, the days are equally handsome.

Srijesh got up from bed furiously, knowing it might be too late. "Chotu get up, it is six already." And he kicked his ass.

Chotu could hardly open his eyes. His hair was straightened which implied he had gone for an intense sleep where there was no place for dream. He wiped the saliva flowing outside his mouth and spoke in a rough voice, "What is the time?"

"Hey, get up. We are late, train must be reaching now."

"My God and it will take at least forty five minutes to Vosco Station from here," Chotu spoke after seeing the watch. They took mere five minutes to get ready.

"Where is the bike key? I am not getting it."

"Search in the bike Bhaiya, Guru keeps there most of the time."

"Got it, come first."

First kick, second kick, third . . . it didn't get started.

If one thing gets wrong, it follows one by one subsequently.

"What is the problem?"

"Arey Bhaiya. Switch it on first."

Srijesh realized the bike is in switch off mode. Suju's bike is a 1995 model moped but rough and tough properly maintained. While Chotu occupied the back seat Srijesh put the first gear on and the bike took off to fourth in less than fifty meter distance. Chotu felt the roar when speedometer touched 100km within few seconds.

"Bhaiya, either I die or the bike is going to get blast. Please ride slowly."

Thank God, it was early morning with less rush. The roads were visible till the capacity of eyesight. But ears turned almost deaf when bike produced the scariest noise in its topmost speed.

"Fucker, it happened because of you." And Srijesh started blaming Chotu.

"Accha, it is because of me!"

"Yes, if we are not reaching on time, I am gonna kill you."

"Arey Bhaiya, forget about you. If we don't reach on time, Guru will fuck me for sure."

"Then why the hell you didn't get up on time."

"Accha, why the hell I didn't get up on time? You tell, why the hell you didn't allow me to sleep? Who kept on asking me about Bengali girls, their look etc. etc. huh?"

"Oh . . . and you are innocent fellow. Who the hell started about Dutta's wife, perfect figure? It is you you you. It is only because of you." And Srijesh rolled the accelerator to maximum making the speedometer crossed beyond speed limit.

"Bhaiya. I beg you. Please have mercy. Oh God, this fellow has gone mad, please save your son." Chotu screamed repeatedly but could not normalize Srijesh. At last he realized there is no point of screaming and finally surrendered by closing his eyes tightly. The velocity of the wind brought tears in their eyes and Chotu laid his head on Srijesh's shoulder skipping all hopes for life. Fortunately they reached Vosco Station and rushed inside the platform.

"No crowd at all. What happened? Whether everybody left in ten-fifteen minutes?"

"Impossible, let me enquire." Srijesh smartly answered by giving an angry look to Chotu but got calm down when he came to know that the train is running late. They both sat on the waiting section and one can observe few common things apart from sheer desperation on their face. It was a deep breath and a sigh of relief.

After ten minutes of wait. No improvement.

Twenty minutes. No sign of arrival.

After thirty minutes. Train is running late by another forty five minutes. Expected time of arrival is 8.30 am.

"This is heights man."

Chotu kept mum and simply smiled. His only intention was to tease Srijesh as he has got enough screwing for their delay in reaching station. And the heroic bike riding of Srijesh went in vain. And so did Srijesh's excitement faint during this hasty waiting session.

"Bhaiya, have patience. The fruit of patience is always sweet."

"Oh stop it man. I am having no more interest to see your Bengali girls. So just chill."

"Ha ha. Very funny. The curiosity is clearly visible in your eyes."

"And if it doesn't get fulfilled, you are going to have it from me."

"Bhaiya. Why are you worried? Just wait and watch." Chotu is expert in beating around the bush and an epitome of overconfidence. But friends consider this as one of his major strengths.

Before Srijesh could ask Chotu to take the final feedback from enquiry office, final announcement was heard. "Howrah Express coming from Howrah to Vosco, which was running late, is arriving shortly at platform number one. We regret for the inconvenience caused to the passengers. Thank you." Chotu jumped from the chair; though Srijesh had lost some energy got at least some striking heartbeat after hearing the announcement. Now the train looked visible, the long waiting sound became highly audible, crowd gathered in the platform and Vosco Station looked bouncy again. It was Christmas special train and Chotu was amazed to see the rush inside. Srijesh turned fretful by thinking they might get jingled with the crowd and won't be able to search the guests. But Chotu has practiced of carrying a customized board where it was written this time, "Mr. Sumit Chaterjee, welcome to Goa."

And he along with Srijesh stood near to a place which looked noticeable from all corners of the platform. The Iron wheel stood still as the train reached the destination place. It was almost five minutes and all the passengers were trying to evacuate in matchless hurries. And suddenly a lean, fair guy appeared infront of Chotu's white board.

"Yeah, from Parker's Hotel. I am Sumit Chaterjee," he said with a voice of higher shrillness.

"Oh, hello sir. I am Chotu and he is . . ."

"Ok, ok. No time for introduction."

Chotu was interrupted in between and asked to follow.

"Getting late, let's go." Chaterjee told by giving an ignorant look to Chotu, typically the way customers react to an ordinary waiter.

"Follow me; we are in front of S8." and his walk & voice, both sound like pure effeminate.

Chotu and Srijesh looked each other surprisingly and followed Chaterjee thoughtlessly. Srijesh didn't like the fact at all that he is getting a response like a hotel boy. "They can be judgemental about Chotu, but how can they consider me?" He kept on asking himself. Chaterjee led both of them to S8 boggy without looking back, where others were waiting for them. Though Parthoda and Banku didn't greet them but gave at least a petty smile.

"Where are the girls?"

"They are getting ready and will take some more time," Banku replied to Chaterjee.

"Getting ready." Srijesh and Chotu looked shocked at each other. "Now what is making them to get ready? Are they going to party? Somebody please tell them, it is Vosco Station and not the night club," Chotu whispered to Srijesh. And finally the impatient wait was over. Among the crowd few girls started coming out one by one. It was Chandrima who stepped out first. A body of heavy weight walking like a jumbo elephant. Srijesh looked from top to bottom and took a sharp turn towards Chotu. He has already lost his confidence after getting a slave like treatment from Chaterjee and above all his expectation got squashed after seeing the heavenly beauty of Chandrima. He wanted to kick Chotu for his blunder projection. He looked at the boggy entrance once again and found a lean, tall but fair girl coming out of the gate. Not so impressive to Srijesh's eyes and he turned completely apathetic.

"Swati. Take your bag."

One fairer girl handed over a vanity bag to Swati, who slowly pushed her towards Chaterjee and started chatting in a manly voice. That girl seems friendlier towards guys and contains an attractive figure with big hips. Chotu considered her name also very big while got to know it. "Si..ban..gi..ni." But the beauty with feminine attitude was still absent in that atmosphere till the last face appeared in front of the group. The girl has worn a pink salwar, who looks shy but confident at the same time. Her eyes looked sleepy but charming. And Srijesh came to know her name as small & simple as her personality, when others asked, "Ritee, shall we start?"

When girls started carrying their respective luggage, Chaterjee refused them like a pure gentleman. He might not resist the luggage to be carried by the sensitive hands of his lady love Swati and hence he said, "Girls, let it be. These two hotel boys will carry it."

Though Chaterjee sounded great to the girls but his words demoted Srijesh to a hotel boy. Poor fellow had come to see some beautiful faces and Suju's assignment turned him into a daily wage labour for that day. He felt mortified but left with no choice when he saw Chotu started doing the job obediently what he has practised to do so. He carried few bags and left few for Srijesh. But unfortunately one of those was Sibangini's, which used to be bumper overweight. He pulled the other one and accidentally the effort made him to hold Ritee's hand instead of the handle of the bag. Though the act was unintentional, it made Ritee to stare at him.

"Oh, sorry," Srijesh told politely.

"No need."

"No, I didn't see it, sorry," Srijesh replied by drawing a little hesitation on his face.

"I am telling, no need to carry the bag. I can take it myself," Ritee told with a firm and strict tone. This short time conversation got interfered by Chaterjee when he asked with an irritating voice, "Hello, Boss, let's go." He actually ordered this to Chotu, knowing he can intimidate him at least, but his response made Srijesh getting highly annoyed.

At last everyone came out of the station. Unlike few days back they saw the cleanest sky when sunrays started hitting the skin. It was 9 am in the morning and a miraculous scene for the folks of Kolkata, who normally feel a thunder cold during this season in their city. Chotu and Srijesh arranged for a vehicle and dumped the luggage inside. Final instruction came to the driver about the boarding point. "Parker's Hotel, Kolva."

The serene greenery was passing by but due to fatigue nobody could enjoy the drive and after almost an hour journey they reached Parker's Hotel where a tall black guy started welcoming the guests.

"Welcome to Goa sir."

"You must be Suju. Prof. Ignesh has told about you."

"Good things or bad things sir."

Chaterjee got blank for a while as he was not expecting a prolonged conversation with Suju.

"Ah . . . yeah. Of course good one, good one."

Suju gradually talked to each of them flawlessly and mingled very quickly. His response even gets bettered while he saw girls got involved in it. Suju even bargained with the taxi driver and convinced him for half of the price what he had quoted earlier. Burning to ashes in jealousy and insecurity, Srijesh and Chotu were in a silent observer list when Suju made the visitors comfortable and invited Chaterjee to see the hotel room.

Parker's Hotel is a two floor mansion looks more like a honeymoon hotel. Typically one night honeymoon deluxe hotel where hardly any married couple comes. But overflows with part-time lovers all the time. One can easily predict after looking at the red colour lightings on the balcony area with 'B' grade pink curtain screen hanging in the window bars. In some balcony, sexy bras and panties looked conspicuous being hanged in drier rope. The inside decoration can definitely arouse the guys if they have not come with families or relatives. Similarly Chaterjee felt a sensation inside heart but his mind didn't allow fitting the known girls in this kind of hotel room. Chaterjee fainted for a while and looked terrified. Privately, he started cursing Prof. Ignesh who has deputed Suju for the convenience of his guests, which is resulting as a disaster. His nervousness prompted him to ask, "Suju, I hope this place is safe for girls."

"Don't misunderstand sir. For girls, we have arranged a separate homestay near to beach and it is just two miles away from here. We will drop them after breakfast," Suju pasted a caring smile and said. Chaterjee could release sufficient breath the moment he got to know that girls will be staying in a better place and his thought of remarks against Prof. Ignesh changed instantly.

Chotu and Srijesh got amazed by the slavery of Suju but this act has already moulded the guests in such a way that they have given permission to Suju to accompany the girls to Parker's Homestay. Quite amazing. Srijesh and Chotu kept their temperament cool against Suju's behaviour as they were getting a chance to spend some more time with the girls. Guests had their surplus breakfast and were guided towards Parker's Homestay thereafter. Chaterjee joined them as a watchdog to monitor his ladylove Swati.

Like a home away from home, Parker's Homestay was a different view all together for the guests when they entered the main gate and a lovely rose garden genially welcomed them. Influenced by Portuguese architecture, the house is made of solid stone inside an acre land of greenery. Three independent houses getting interconnected with a narrow lane demarcated with small size bricks on a grassy surface. One small pool situated exactly in the junction where two white swans play all the time in between few Lilies. With plenty of trees inside the compound, one can hardly believe three houses coexist. Girls were astonished to see the outstanding natural beauty inside the premise and they completely forgot the pain of their journey. It was not only the beauty which attracted them but something their eyes had never seen before. And looking at this composed scenario, Chaterjee had already climbed to a state of day dream about Swati along with his adult fantasy.

They all proceeded towards the guest house and Suju opened the wooden door lock. Nobody except Chotu knows from where he got the key. The house is loaded with wooden furniture and parabola like roof made of raw stone gives immense cool even in hot climate.

Awesome,

Lovely,

Fantastic.

These few words from the guests definitely launched a rocket of motivation to Suju who disclosed each and every aspects and amenities of the house, which one can expect only the owner should know. But was Suju different? Not at all. He has successfully utilized all the places and props inside this house with his girlfriend. And that is why he is rewarded with a prize, one spare house key for entertainment.

Bengal beauties started speaking in the air while trying to resist the exquisite view of the interior. But it was not over yet. At last they saw the roof top compound from where one can enthral the stunning view of Kolva Beach. It will be no wrong to express in one word, "Heaven."

"Ok madams, if you need anything at any point of time, don't trouble yourself to call me."

"What nonsense, what this fellow is telling?" Srijesh asked Chotu in a strange voice. And the guests got surprise as well.

Suju smiled and said, "Madams, I am just joking. Don't worry. My two assistants are there always at your service and my house is also nearby. You can disturb them at any point of time. And they will never disobey your orders." Suju has become out of reach now from Srijesh's mercy. He along with Chotu has already planned to prank him tonight if he does not refund their lost respect. Without wasting any more time, Suju took Chaterjee who is a happy man now after seeing the special escort offered to the girls. And finally the moment came for a fraction of time when guests were left with Srijesh and Chotu. They both were not able to speak anything bearing their reluctance. Perhaps they are not smart as Suju, neither Suju has left any topics of discussion and covered everything in his good bye speech. So like unwanted members they both were coming out of the house, by then a voice interrupted them with the help of its naive question.

"Exxxxcuse me, where can we get food in the lunch time?" Innocent Chandrima dared to ask them. Srijesh turned back while all were looking at him as if he is a saviour. Though it was one voice, he came to know it was actually representing everyone's feeling.

"No issue, we will inform the owner's cook to prepare food. But there is one problem; you might get only Western food. But if you prefer Indian, then we will arrange catering for you," Srijesh replied like a true saviour.

Girls started murmuring in Bengali to confuse them, but Chotu realized that he got a role to play.

"Whether we will get Indian food?" Sibangini asked.

"Or Bengali food," Chandrima asked once again with fingers scratching her head.

"It is okay. Any meals will be fine." Finally Ritee spoke like a mature one from the squad.

"Okay, we will send. 1 o' clock will be fine I believe."

"Oh yes. So nice of you," Chandrima replied with a grin on her face as she got a timely confirmation of lunch. Immediately she took out a twenty rupee note and tried to handover it to Srijesh, but it was Chotu who extended his palm.

"No, no, it is not required now. You can give against the bill," Srijesh said after tapping Chotu's feet to signal a negative approval for taking money.

"It is not for food. It is for you both, keep it," Chandrima answered politely.

"A tip. What these girls think about me. Am I a servant? This all happened because of Suju Uncle. I will not spare him," and he turned furious while talking to himself.

"Madam, we don't take tips. We will send the lunch before one. Have a good day." He pulled Chotu and they both left the place. Neither had he taken nor did he allow Chotu to take the money which upset poor Chotu lethally.

By then Srijesh and Chotu came out of the campus, Srijesh looked heated and asked him, "Why the hell you were about to take the money beggar?"

"And why the hell you didn't allow me to collect it great man?" Chotu exchanged a question in reply.

"All are the daughters of some rich fathers and showing off. Let them piss off. I won't come here again."

"Ok, ok, I will deliver. Don't panic." And chotu smiled.

"Now why are you smiling?"

"I am smiling because of your innocence."

"Means?"

"Arey Bhaiya. They ordered South Indian meals instead of Western food having realized it might come cheaper. And you think they are rich brat." Chotu smiled again.

7

$\mathcal{I}$t was a slow-moving afternoon in Parker's Hotel when guests were in search of Suju. Perhaps they were in need of something which only Suju was capable to arrange for.

"You need something sir," Chotu asked by looking at the aimless movement of Chaterjee.

"Yeah . . . huh, no just leave it. Ask Suju to meet us once he comes," said Chaterjee and left from there.

"What is his problem man?" And Chotu gave a staggered look.

"You didn't get. Perhaps they are searching for liquor. Whether Bengali people drink?" Srijesh asked.

Chotu laughed loudly and replied, "DRINK. What a joke. Bhaiya, they drink like anything. Haven't you heard about Devdas?"

"Who?"

"Arey Devdas, a rich Bengali guy, who sacrificed his life for drinking," Chotu explained as if he has personally witnessed his death.

"Sacrificed his life. Oh . . . you are talking about that Devdas. What nonsense? That is a story man."

"Is it?" Chotu squeezed his eyes.

"Chotu, you blamed me enough for your loss of tip. Do you want some extra income?"

"Yes. But how?"

"I am sure these people are voraciously looking for drinks. Just go and hike your prices for fifty rupees at least. You will get much more than you lost. Go."

"Wow Bhaiya. You didn't take a single penny from the girls and you are in a mood to loot these guys. Very smart, huh. Let me try." Chotu anxiously approached towards Chaterjee.

"Sir, do you require some snacks?"

"Yes, yes."

"Along with some cool drinks."

"Yeah."

"Little bit of Soda."

"Of course."

"Beer or whisky sir?"

"Whiskey, one full bottle."

"Great, total four fifty rupees sir."

"Four hundred and fifty, how?"

Chotu became speechless as he could not detail the calculation and lost all hopes of earning. But a voice rose from behind and it was Parthoda's.

"Ok, bring it faster and inform Suju to come." And he handed over Rs. 500 instead of Rs 450.

Chotu hopped upto Srijesh and told over one breath.

"Arey Bhaiya. While girls are not ready to spend much, this fellow is throwing money like anything." Chotu is delighted and went unstoppable to liquor shop.

During evening the moonlight arose to overpower the colourful lighting of the streets in Kolva. People came out of their houses and the streets looked lively. Somewhere there was foot tapping music and somewhere beautiful songs kept the atmosphere busy. Houses looked cheerful and people in a mood of joy. Kolva started looking young once again. And the version of celebration for the guests in Parker's Hotel, was to drink tightly till the late evening.

Suju calls it a VIP lounge where he took the Bengali guests to the terrace. He arranged few chairs and made a homey atmosphere under the umbrella shaped bamboo roof. It looks made exclusively for drinking purpose and Suju normally invites female foreign tourists to bring their attraction to this place. Guests occupied their respective seats and Chotu brought few glasses before Suju could order him. Parthoda seemed to be in his altruistic and caring self as he invited Chotu and Srijesh too. Suju made the pegs and all raised the toast. "To Goa." While the hosts were taking gentle sips, Parthoda and Banku finished their respective glasses in one shot.

"Whether Bengalis drink this way?" a surprised Srijesh whispered to chotu's ear which he wisely answered, "I told you about Devdas, must be their ancestor."

A drunken Parthoda appreciated the hosts after receiving the world class hospitality. Entire day he has hardly spoken but the drink brought out all his emotions. Others too felt the real taste of Goa being present that night. The cosy evening, winter breeze and the drinks escalated the visitors to a vintage.

"Ok boys. Just take it away and clean it," a drunken Chaterjee ordered Chotu.

"No need sir. I will call the servants," Suju told.

"Yeah, I am speaking to them only."

"No sir, the mistake is mine. I have not introduced them properly. They both are not servants. These two are my family in Goa," Suju said after putting hands on Chotu's and Srijesh's shoulder. And chaterjee laughed by thinking, Suju is drunk completely.

"You are great Suju. I think you are completely boozed."

"Sir, these two three pegs are nothing for me. If I start drinking, I count only bottles and not the pegs. But whatever I am telling now is completely true. Chotu is like my brother and Srijesh is my own nephew. He is a post graduate from Goa University. They both are helping me just to make you comfortable sir; else they are nothing to do with it," Emotional Suju replied in teary eyes along with pride in his voice. May be post graduate was the optimum degree for his understanding. And Chotu and Srijesh realized, "He is completely drunk." But this emotional speech made the guest dumbstruck for a moment and Chaterjee to stand up from his chair.

"Oh. We are sorry brother. We didn't know at all." Chaterjee's words were bursting with shame.

They all had dinner together and Chaterjee requested Suju to carry food parcel for the girls. He even got exposed towards his hidden love for Swati in front of all, while drinking. Suju took a round of the hotel as a part of his daily routine and left along with Chotu and Srijesh to Parker's Homestay.

It was 9.30 pm in the evening at Parker's home and nobody has slept till now due to Christmas season.

"Come guys. I will introduce you to Parker family." And Suju pulled both of them towards the door entry.

Chotu told stitching a little smile on his face, "Now Guru will introduce his in laws. Come, let's go."

"Bugger, don't try to be over smart. I will drill your asshole."

"All yours." Chotu bent his waist towards Suju.

"Uncle, we'll wait here. You finish your formalities and come back."

"Bhaiya, it's better to leave. You can't wait as his formality is not going to get finished at least for two hours, if he meets his out dated girlfriend." He meant Ms. Parker's mother who was on a bedtime relationship with Suju.

After few seconds of gate knock an old lady appeared and gave a greeting smile to Suju but like a stranger to Chotu and Srijesh. Looking at her reaction one can assume the welcome would have been entire different, if Suju would have come alone. She looks triple the size of Suju but seems very strong from appearance. Chotu and Srijesh wanted to commend Suju for his brave selection of playmate. Nevertheless she asked everyone to come inside.

"So she is . . . ?" Srijesh tried to ask the big question to Chotu after recognizing the old lady.

"You are correct Bhaiya. She is the one. Guru's girlfriend. Looking hot. Isn't she?"

"Hot or completely burnt?" They both started giggling.

"Very true. Look at her night gown?"

"Yeah, looking beautiful. But is there anything special?"

"Look properly, no bra."

"Yes man. Yours is an owl's eye Chotu. She has not put on her bra."

"Correct your statement Bhaiya. No bra can be put on to withstand 52 sizes of heavy balls."

Both started chewing their inner cheeks to control their laughter.

"Who are they?" The old lady tried to intimidate Suju by seeing the childish response from Chotu and Srijesh. Suju introduced one another and sent Chotu and Srijesh to parcel the food for girls. Perhaps he wanted to spend some intimate seconds with his girlfriend till others come.

Chotu and Srijesh went to the guest house and pressed the calling bell. They heard some beautiful songs being sung by the girls which got disconnected immediately after the bell rang.

"Yes." And Swati opened the door.

"Ms. Swati."

"Yes, I am." And all gathered in front of the door. Unlike Suju's girlfriend, they were in full sleeve dresses even in the night which upset Chotu.

"Chaterjee sir has sent the food parcel," he said.

"Only for me."

"No, it is for all. But he asked us to handover it especially to you," Srijesh replied smartly and all the girls started teasing Swati which turned her redden for a while. Girls gave a thanking note to Srijesh and Chotu, while they were about to leave.

"Hey, Srijesh. Come here," Suju cried from Parker's house and when Srijesh approached there he saw the entire Parker family waiting for him especially.

"I am sure, Uncle would have done some overacting and that is why I am so curiously being waited." Srijesh realized and entered the porch of the house.

Ms. Parker's husband, their twin sons and the mother in law were speaking to one another while a beautiful lady came out of the house with a guitar in hand. She is none other than Ms. Parker herself. A meaty brown skin looks like pulpy orange with flesh in appropriate proportion in her body. She looks like an angel, especially if someone sees her after drinking. Moreover the red colour velvet gown on her body was enhancing her beauty up to the peak. Chotu got lubricated and started imagining her without bra.

"Something to cheer for Christmas," Ms. Parker asked him to play a song while handing over the guitar and entire family started cheering for Srijesh. Suju also encouraged him in a compelling way to compose a fine tune. The twin brothers started clapping for their teacher till Srijesh could concentrate for few words to sing. Even though no words were coming to his mind he obeyed them.

"Someday I will be yours

Someday you will be mine

I am waiting for the time

The day will be of mine."

The song played in unison with the guitar. Hardly a minute of composition but it was worthy for all to be patient enough and listen to it. He did miracle with some fine tunes of guitar which was coming from his heart. Everyone went amazed with the sweet music and the intensity of clap got multiplied when the girls joined into the listeners list. For the Bengal beauties it was truly an incredible ambiance when they saw the unreasonable celebrations, music, gentle breeze of Kolva Beach, beautiful people and twin little Parker Brothers.

"Superb, fabulous." The owners started complementing Srijesh and Suju took the position of a host when he announced, "This was for the beautiful Parker family and now for the beauty of Bengals."

Srijesh felt like Suju was helping his inner feelings to make it reachable to the girls. A deep silence of expectation surrounded there. No clap so far. And the miracle happened once again when Srijesh started playing the tune of a Bengali song which he merely heard few minutes ago at the guest house. The girls thoroughly enjoyed and went crazy about the music. Their joy knew no bounds as they tapped their feet harder till the composition ran. A drunken Suju took the opportunity to invite everyone for a dance. Girls started exposing their freedom and participated in dance which overtook the music for a while. They started interacting with Srijesh like affable companion and praised him. "Your music was fantastic," and it sounded like they were thanking him for creating a beautiful evening. The day had not been good for Srijesh so far but the evening was truly a memorable one. He concluded while leaving for his house.

8

$\mathcal{S}$econd day was supposed to be occupied for the city tour. Considering Prof. Ignesh's engagement followed by marriage ceremony from tomorrow onwards, visitors wanted to wrap off the schedule as quick as possible. Girls slept tightly yesterday to preserve maximum energy for city tour; however Srijesh on the other hand could not stop thinking about last night. His eyes were stuck to a face that looks pretty conservative, simple yet sensible and a smile like a child. She is known as 'Ritee' by her friends. He kept on thinking if the girl has noticed him the way he has presented himself. He waited for today patiently. Suju, the mastermind wanted to write some brilliant scripts for Srijesh and the initials of his love life. He has already arranged a vehicle and sent Srijesh along with Chotu, as a guide to the visitors. Leaving Chaterjee, he convinced Banku and Parthoda to opt out of the city tour. Probably he brainwashed them and gave some exciting offers of entertainment meant only for bachelor guys.

Day started and the girls were eagerly waiting for the city tour to begin. Srijesh and Chaterjee along with Chotu brought the vehicle and waited for them at the front gate of Parker's Homestay. It was close to 11 in the morning and girls came out of their guest house to visit the mesmerizing Goa they have heard about. By looking at their way of dressing, one can clearly state that they are not yet aligned to the quintessential charm of Goa. All have worn their traditional salwar kameej. But amongst all it was Ritee who looks like a fresh bird. Jasmine colour salwar and a pink chunri. Her long hair was pressed hard and was knotted by a red colour ribbon. Her black colour bindi looked appealing to the eyes of Srijesh. And he felt the assuasive smell of lavender fragrance when she came closer to the vehicle. Looking at the girls, Chotu could only remember the advertisement of Santoor soap aired in television.

42

"Where are Parthoda and Banku?" Chandrima showed some concern and asked.

"They are still sleeping being drunk heavily last night."

"And you?"

"Have you seen me drinking? I never do that." Chaterjee started the day with a lie to impress Swati.

"Would you like to wait for them?"

"No, it's ok. Let's go."

The above answer from girls gave a boost to Srijesh and Chotu as they realized that girls are now comfortable to travel with them. But Srijesh is unaware about the impression he has left last night which has changed his image as more than an acquaintance to the girls.

"Hello Mr. Musician," a chatty Sibangini greeted Srijesh to bring a blush on his face.

All got settled and the journey accelerated along with typical boy girl conversation with amusing gestures. The city tour seems like a readymade menu. Chotu and Srijesh have accompanied few tourists for the same activity before and have got fed up. They have to show the same Secretariat, Fort, Museum and City market. Nothing one can add nor delete. Similar to readymade meals, neither you can put some add-ons nor you can withdraw any items. Nevertheless they are honest to their duties and started finishing one by one. It will be boredom if girls would not have been there. And the small love story between Swati and Chatrejee was working like icing on the cake.

They halted the journey in their first destination spot 'Secretariat' and the reaction came from girls was, "Ahh, Kolkata secretariat is much bigger than this one."

The second spot was the Fort for which girls placed a remark, "This one is nothing. Kolkata palace is far better than this one."

And the third one was Museum which the girls pointed as, "Average, if you see Kolkata museum, it will be nowhere."

Even though all these irate reactions began hurting his over possessiveness towards Goa, Srijesh managed to keep his temperament unruffled for a while.

"What Chaterjee, to show these places you came a long way to Goa? This could have been done in Kolkata man." Sibangini burst some derogatory remarks and girls started laughing at it. Chaterjee became dumb and didn't mind at all as he was busy in watching Swati's cute smile.

"What do you say Mr. Chotu, have you been to Kolkata?"

"Yes madam, I too agree. East or west. Kolkata is the best." Chotu did the same what he has learnt from his Guru. "Customer is the king and you have to dance naked to its tune." He started praising Kolkata even though he has never been there before. But his cheek swelled when Sibangini told him, "Wow. Well said Brother." Chotu hates if some girls call him as Brother.

"And you Mr. Musician, where and all you are taking us now?" Sibangini the talkative now tried to throw her comments to Srijesh. And Srijesh, who was feeling the burn in his heart by these humiliations, was trying his best to overcome the stretch from his forehead. But his honesty overpowered his tolerance and he forcibly replied, "Nowhere. Absolutely nowhere."

"What?"

"Trust me; there is no point of going anywhere, if you people behave super judgmental."

A scared Sibangini could tell only one formal word, "Sorry."

"No, truly. You are wasting your time by randomly visiting these places just for the sake of going. I mean, don't compare. Your city might be the best. But this place is having its own identity. Don't ruin it please."

After few seconds of silence, Ritee took the initiative to cool down the atmosphere. "We are sorry, we know how it hurts if somebody tells against your native. But we didn't mean it really." The same chauvinism even she constitutes for her native, what she beheld in Srijesh's voice.

"Don't be. What I am trying to say is, if you really want to see Goa, just pour yourself to its colour. There is much more what this place can offer but only when you make yourself truly of this paradise." And Srijesh's obsession for Goa reflected strongly through his words.

"Okay Mr. Musician, so now it is your turn. Just throw these crap places from your city tour menu. Be our pilot and take us through your favourite places." Ritee sounded more matured and Srijesh got totally convinced to this girl's uniqueness. He quite liked it. He was numb for a while before Ritee reiterated.

"Yeah, tell then, where you are going to take us?"

"I think I should take you to a restaurant first, else you people will eat me in lunch for sure." All started laughing at Srijesh's sense of humour and the hot atmosphere of discussions got marginally abated.

"Now you decide which type of restaurant you wanna go? North India, Chinese, South Indian, Bengali . . ."

"Nope . . . Goan, typical Goan." Sibangini and Ritee replied in one voice. Srijesh got encouraged as girls started buying his melodies.

"Why the girls are calling him a musician?" A duped Chaterjee asked Chotu.

"Sir, I think you are hungry. Let's go."

After a tardy first half of the day, they entered into a fine dine Goan restaurant. It is a known restaurant to Srijesh and he is known to the staffs as well. He was greeted by the doorman and waiter asked for the order, the moment they occupied the table.

"You may ask our guest." Srijesh told by pointing his hand towards Chaterjee.

Chaterjee haphazardly picked few dishes and tried to order but the waiter could not make out his accent. Neither could he make out when others struggled to place the order.

"Gentleman, three plates each Prawns and Fish Xacuti, White Rice four plates and Yellow Dal. Two Chapatti each for everyone followed by dessert." Srijesh ordered in a handsome phonetics and girls got amazed. Now girls were bound to think more about this guy.

"I mean, we just want to know more about you." Sibangini reinforced their thought and Chaterjee replied with a smile.

"Girls, let me introduce you Mr. Srijesh. He is a master of Social Science from Goa University. Never judge by his politeness, we all are misinterpreted. He is just guiding to make us comfortable."

"And he is a musician too," Ritee said.

"Really." And they tried to know more about one another. That is where the friendship began and their actual journey started in Goa.

They spent the next few hours in Kolva Beach which used to be amply crowded. Even though it was not in the plan of city tour, Srijesh took them knowing a daily life in Goa is incomplete if it is not concluded on the sea shore. Girls could feel the burning of tiredness after stamping their feet in sea water. They were sprinting like small children, playing with the sea sand and behaving like free birds. But amongst all it was Ritee who completely captivated the attention of Srijesh and by looking at her, he could feel peace even inside the intense noise of Christmas Eve.

During late evening Chaterjee got down in hotel but gave the responsibility to Srijesh for dropping the girls in Parker's Homestay. It was almost 9 o' clock in the watch when he dropped all of them and girls thanked him for offering one more memorable evening. Girls entered inside their guest house but Srijesh's heart was rendering for Ritee to look back once. He fettered his feet and watched Ritee for some more time.

"Bhaiya, let's go." Chotu called him at the end.

9

$\mathcal{I}$t was the auspicious Christmas day and the day of engagement. It was one of the important days for which the Bengalis have come to Goa. Engagement between Prof. Ignesh Fernandes and Silviya Pinto. Two of the well-known families of Goa have booked a royal party hall in the mid of Margaon city. Whosoever was invited to the engagement, believed this would be one of the biggest functions in the city; however the true stature was unknown to the visitors. All seven members had to attend this one. This time even Parthoda and Banku were in the list of active attendants as they had to oblige the rapport between them and Prof. Ignesh. But there lies one more supporting factor. It is evident that drinks will be abundantly available being a royal Christian party.

They entered the hall and went spellbound after looking at the lavish decoration.

"My God, if this is the situation in engagement, what would be in marriage?" A mesmerized Swati asked everyone.

"Very true." And Chaterjee did his job of a pet.

"How am I looking?" An anxious Sibangini was seeking some compliments while she whispered the question to Ritee. Unlike others, Sibangini has put on a yellow sari as she wanted to look special. Probably she was craving for a look of sexy lady that evening to woo Prof. Ignesh.

"You are looking beautiful my dear and your face look so sweet."

"Hey come on. I am not asking about my face. What about the other parts?" Sibangini asked and started setting her sari fall above her blouse.

Ritee could not respond anything but a smile.

"I know. I am looking like a stupid. Neither my face looks glowing nor is this sari looks transparent to catch his attention."

"No I promise, you are looking super-hot."

47

"Hah. Shut up. The lie is truly getting reflected in your tone. I only want to look more beautiful than his fiancé. That's it. I am sure she will be an ugly duckling. Let Professor see me once. I want his ass to burn if he compares me with his would be wife."

"Oh stop it Sibangini. He is getting married."

"Oho, you seem very happy. I believe you are also enjoying the party."

"No dear, I am feeling bore."

"Okay. I know why it is for?"

"Oh really, my intelligent friend, why it is for?"

"Because your eyes are looking for someone and Mr. Musician is not visible to it."

"I will beat you Sibangini." Ritee pressed her jaws to control anger but Sibangini's words made her realize that she is mentally not present in the party. Also she is not feeling the same excitement like yesterday and something is really missing for her. Is it what Sibangini meant?

"No no, not at all. And I don't think he will be coming," Ritee said and tried to avoid the clumsy eye contact from Sibangini.

"Yes, I told you. You are actually thinking about him." Sibangini needled her as she wanted to take her friend to the same ride of falling in love.

"Arey, I saw that small boy here. He was roaming somewhere here. Yeah there he is. Hey, hero. Come." Sibangini signalled and raised her hands towards Chotu.

"How are you hero?"

"Very busy. You know, this entire catering is outsourced to us." Chotu carried pride while introducing.

"Ohho, great. By the way, where is your musician brother?"

"Who? Oh, Srijesh Bhaiya. Don't ask . . . some problem with him. Neither he is able to sleep nor is he taking his food properly." May be Chotu knew their covert intention of asking about Srijesh. And this small boy's answer made Sibangini to a jaw dropping reactions.

"Is it true? That means, hearts are burning from both the sides," Sibangini murmured something in Bengali and got a slap from Ritee in return.

By looking at the girls' reactions, Chotu started laughing inside. He can make out their gossip and he realized his words of exaggeration have done the application of a medicine. He wanted to speak to the girls for some more time but decided to leave after seeing the host family entering the hall. Girls didn't stop him as they got to see Prof. Ignesh coming. Especially Sibangini whose smiley face became red and palpable nervousness appeared on it. By looking at the Bengali guests, Professor slowly approached towards them along with an old but stylish lady who looked like his mother. That day Prof. Ignesh was looking like a tall, dark and handsome man who can misguide any beautiful women present in the party. Once again Sibangini felt magnetized by his virile personality. Being a true gentleman he thanked his students who have come a long way to attend his marriage. He introduced all of them to his mother and conveyed his high regards to them. All greeted his mother with folded hands but there happened a shocking experience when Sibangini touched her feet. While others got stunned, Mother greeted Sibangini with a kiss on her forehead. Before the situation becomes little awkward, Professor took over and started being courteous once again.

"Really friends. Thank you all for coming. I owe a big time to you both. Chaterjee, Swati, you both have to participate in all the functions as my closest friends."

Chaterjee and Swati got overwhelmed after receiving this kind of congeniality from Prof. Ignesh. They used to be his favourite students in college. And after getting this kind of response, they have already assumed of their final year lab practical marks to be cent percent. They followed him near to the stage which made Sibangini getting separated. She felt departed but Ritee held her trembled hands like a true friend in need.

"Look at these bloody traitors," Sibangini got furious and pointed at Swati and Chaterjee.

"Let them be dear. Calm down," Ritee started consoling her.

After few minutes the ring exchange ceremony started. Both families got united when the proud parents, relatives came on the stage. The atmosphere was looking more than just an engagement ceremony, rather looking like a coalition ceremony of two big political parties. The loud speaker & music kept on beating the hearts and were pumping up everyone's breath. The announcement started and Mr. Fernandes, the head of the family introduced his would be daughter in law by instructing all to put on their hands for the beautiful, the gorgeous Ms. Silviya Pinto. All eyes were waiting for the lucky lady to appear on to the stage but nobody would be more curious to see her than Sibangini who was impatiently waiting for the lady and to detest her being prejudiced. She was praying for an ugly face to be unveiled on the stage; however the end result became entirely opposite. A stunning beauty appeared in a red colour sari. She looked ultra-fair blended with a flawless skin. The rosy diamond necklace was giving a strong complement to the lovely face. Five feet eight inches of gorgeous figure and a scintillating smile of the heart shape face were titillating all the guys to get envious to Prof. Ignesh. But any sensible person, present in the ceremony, will be telling only one sentence from their hearts undoubtedly and so does Ritee.

"Wow, what a lovely pair these both make," Ritee said though she knows Sibangini is standing beside her. May be it jumped out automatically, similar to the majority of attendants. But this made her scared of looking at Sibangini immediately.

And finally the main event started. The couple started exchanging the rings, the purple solitaire. Now the stage was enveloped by the near and dears of both the families along with a portion occupied by the Bengali students. The moment they could exchange the rings, an unknown voice struck everyone's ear from the crowd.

"Now you may kiss the bride."

Though it sounded little absurd in the first stroke, it became a chorus after few seconds. This was making the couple being melted with blush. They looked at each other with shy and made a romantic eye contact for a while. These all moments were like a spark of magic for Ritee who has never seen it before. She started enjoying it leaving behind the emotional drama of Sibangini. But before she could swing herself into these lovely moments, she got distracted by Sibangini's break out. Sibangini started weeping for the sake of her broken heart leading to an impossible attempt for Ritee to console. She could smell the slow smouldering jealously in Sibangini after observing the visceral chemistry between Professor and his fiancé.

"Oh my God. Baby please, don't cry."

She couldn't wish a miracle to happen which might dilute Sibangini's grief immediately, but she needed someone to share her effort in bringing back a smile on her friend's face. And Srijesh came towards them to be a joker. Even for him it was impossible to believe, a carefree girl like Sibangini is crying in the mid of the lively function where there is no space for any boredom. He couldn't empathize but chose to ask her for the reason at least. He sat on the chair beside her and enquired.

"Any problem, why is she?"

"A long story. Could you please take us out of this place?" Ritee didn't know how she could ask Srijesh passively, but it just came out from her mouth uncertain.

"Now . . . are you sure?"

"Yes. Please."

"Do you know the loneliest place in Goa?" Sibangini asked him as if she wanted to commit suicide there. She looked distorted.

And after a few minutes of mind reading, Srijesh took them out of the function and brought them in to the most silent church in Benaulim. In Christmas day, the church was decorated with lightings and people were assembled for the evening prayer. Ritee and Sibangini had hardly been to a church before and got the opportunity to see it closer. They realized the calmness of this place and felt the presence of God. While other people were walking on the pavement outside the church, Srijesh handed over two candles to Sibangini and Ritee and said, "You may light on and ask your wishes to God."

"Ok, I will take it." After telling so Sibangini entered inside the church to light up the candle.

"And you believe, whatever we ask, God will give it to us," Ritee told and looked at him. She looked convincing and seeking for the truth. But neither Srijesh was having an answer for that nor did he want to break Ritee's belief by keeping a silence. And he replied firmly, "Yes, I do believe."

"Huh." Ritee set an agnostic smile.

"Ok. Just look at your friend. While praying God, she started believing herself. I am sure, even if she doesn't get her wishes; she will generate enough strength to earn it."

Ritee took a glance at Sibangini and suddenly turned towards Srijesh. This time Srijesh's look was not like a stranger. May be he wanted to say few more words but chained himself to his limits. He gave a persuasive smile and lightened up her candle which made Ritee to close her eyelid. Without looking at Srijesh, she walked away and prayed for a while. And Srijesh could not take his eyes off while seeing Ritee bending down on her knees and folded hands. Her prayer looks innocent and selfless as if she doesn't seek anything for her, but for others. Her way of praying was not typically the way people do in church but the devotion she carried was more than many of them. Srijesh kept on questioning him, "Why am I so involved to look at her? How can she look so beautiful? Is it because of her innocence blended with it? Oh God, let me turn around before she can point out me noticing."

He dropped them safely to Parker's Homestay before situation gets disturbed if others find their absence for a long time. But Srijesh never believed that he will get one more opportunity to spend time with them, as Sibangini asked him.

"Excuse me. What are you doing tomorrow?"

"Nothing much. Why?" Srijesh replied briskly as he understood their core intent.

"Can you just take us few more good places of Goa?"

"Sure." Srijesh gave a flat reply but inwardly he was controlling his excitement.

"But it must be nearby," Ritee said.

10

$\mathcal{S}$ibangini and Ritee were in their usual smartness. While the former gave a pretext of bad health, the later became her caretaker for that day. They skipped to visit Prof. Ignesh's home who has invited them for dinner. And when everybody left, they came out of their premise to spend another evening with Srijesh and the beautiful Goa. Perhaps Srijesh knows, the best way to ail the broken heart of girls is to take them for shopping. They went crazy after looking at the beachside Western market and its speciality. They shopped as per their pocket size and Srijesh was busy in noticing Ritee. The way she eagerly looks at things she wants to buy, the way she bargains with the seller. And finally when she gets something as per her desired price, she shows her cherubic smile of achievement. It was so nice to see her that time. She invited Srijesh to join them, but he politely refused. For him, watching Ritee without her consent was more fun than being with her. He got more enjoyment by instructing her, from the other side of the street, about the choice of her bangles. Ritee could look at the mirror to evaluate but even she textured gladness when Srijesh appraised her with gestures for the choice of her ear rings.

The best way to see Goa is to visit with someone who knows it like its own. And girls felt blessed by roaming with Srijesh to feel its inner beauties. They were introduced to its exotic beaches, colourful country side and the lousy evening. But they felt dumbfounded at a clandestine beach of Benaulim shown by Srijesh. Though it was nowhere mentioned 'a person can forget entire sorrows being in this kind of lonely places' Srijesh still told Sibangini with a sense of assurance, "Don't worry, everything will be fine."

"It is not that easy Srijesh."

"I know this is none of my business, but you should try to share it to others. May be you feel better."

Sibangini looked at Ritee before saying anything, but when her Darling Ritee shook her eyes close that indicated her to open up. She briefed and realized it must abate her sorrows and simultaneously will not give a sigh of regret for disclosing it to a less known friend.

"I loved someone and now he is getting married to someone else. I know that I have to be strong in this crucial hours but my heart is not allowing me to. Because I know, I will not get a better person than him in my entire life."

"Do you believe that the other person loves you the same way you do."

"I don't think so," Sibangini replied.

"Then I am sure, you will get a better person than him in future. Mark my words."

"Huh! Is it written in my face?"

"Well . . . it is written on your palm."

"Is it? How can you tell, as if you are a palm reader?" Sibangini asked with optimum anxiety.

"Yeah, a sort of."

"Really, are you serious? Why didn't you tell us before then?" Poor girl could not comprehend that Srijesh was actually trying to amuse her with some funny tricks. But whatever was his intention; Ritee welcomed it and felt thankful to him. And Sibangini curiously extended her palms.

"Okay, let me tell you, there are few more personal things noticed other than your beautiful palms."

"Ok and what are those?" Sibangini's curiosity mounted further on her smiley face.

And Intelligent Srijesh told merely few sentences for Sibangini which usually most of the people approve for themselves.

"The person, who you love now, is not your first love."

"Yes, it is absolutely correct, how do you know?"

"Ok, secondly, you have got a high potential in you, but you have not taken it seriously neither you have utilized it properly," Srijesh told the sentence while bringing a stretchmark on the forehead to make it look more genuine.

"Yes, I do realize, I have never taken my life seriously. Then what? Shall I get a man who will love me the most? Only me," Sibangini told by showing her distressful face.

"Definitely. It is written in your fate. And nobody can change it. And last but not the least, you don't like gloominess, so let me take you to a place where you will receive the noise of enjoyment. Are you ready?"

These above remarks of Srijesh brought the real Sibangini back and Srijesh realized, what Suju has told him once is absolutely true. Girls believe everything if someone speaks with confidence. And that is what he did today. He planned to take the girls to a beachside open air club to show them the noise of enjoyment. Sibangini found few drops of excitement in this bizarre situation. And Ritee was highly impressed by Srijesh's intelligence which made her to ask, "Your name should be magician." And she gave a thanking note to Srijesh through her words.

"You Bengali girls seem very courteous. No?"

"Aha, why?"

"You thank a person lot many times. Do you do the same especially to your friends?"

"Yes. Obviously," Ritee replied.

"Ok. So now I believe that you consider me as your friend at least."

Ritee smiled as she could clearly point out his wicked boyish orientation.

"See, I didn't do anything to your friend. She is a brave girl undoubtedly. All I can see a soft heart inside her, otherwise it is never easy to forgive the person who hurt you badly."

"My God, you can judge a person so early. I told your name should be magician."

And now Srijesh smiled at Ritee, after seeing a fraction of jealousy on her face. That moment Srijesh understood one more covert truth. Girls normally become jealous if somebody praises their best friends. He even realized girls look pretty and dominant that time, after closely observing Ritee. He continued looking at her as he believed Ritee will not divert her attention being dominant that time. Srijesh wanted to say few more words for her favour before a strong wind blew and distracted their vision. Though Ritee was eager to listen to some nice comments, she could not do much but twirled her strand of hair and kept silent. Sibangini interrupted them as she shouted to convey her hurries to go to places; otherwise Srijesh would have said what he has clamped inside his heart from a long time, "Ritee, you look so beautiful." What an obstacle Sibangini.

Ritee lifted her sandal which she had removed to feel the frigid touch of sea water and started walking. She wanted to be followed by Srijesh and Srijesh on the other hand wanted her to turn back. Her small look can uplift his aroma of strong feelings. And she not only looked back this time but hinted him to come forward and show them the real self of scintillating Goa.

Srijesh escorted them to a known open air night club on the seashore of Kolva Beach. It belongs to one of Suju's closest friends and he comes there frequently. It was Christmas season and every club owners plan for some attractive activities to pull maximum numbers of customers. It was pure fun for Ritee and Sibangini who were asked to apply for the lucky coupons even before entering the club. They came to know, it would take three lucky mascots to the exquisite Blue Lagoon resort which is known as one of the most exciting places of Goa. But the coupon will be available only against the order of today's special Blueberry Mojito.

"Are you sure you want to order it?" Srijesh asked in confusion.

"Yeah, this is the eligibility criteria to be chosen for lucky coupon I believe." Sibangini was willing to try her luck.

"But you know what Mojito means?"

"MOJITO MEANS HEAVEN ON EARTH." A loud voice was heard behind and it was Suju's. "Okay, so the whole attraction is here huh. You people disappeared from yesterday. Is everything alright?" Suju told loudly as he had to compete with the music of the night club to make his voice audible.

"Yeah." And Sibangini chuckled.

"Ok, then. Today's order is from my side. Hey boy, bring three Blueberry Mojitos (with a loud voice) and a glass of vodka (with a soft tone)."

Srijesh knew that they have to listen to some nonsense and matching his expectation Suju restarted, "Let me tell you the universal truth. God has sent two fantastic things on earth. A living and a non living. He sent beautiful girls like you and beautiful Blueberry Mojito."

Srijesh wished if he could speak flawless like Suju. Especially to Ritee. But still he was busy in collecting his strength.

"By the way Uncle, what is special today?"

"You don't know. Do you see that old lady? Today is her ex-husband's death ceremony and she is sponsoring a glass of vodka for each of the attendants," Suju told pointing his finger at a beautiful old lady.

"And she is celebrating . . . ."

"Wait, it is not over yet. Do you see a fellow standing next to her?"

"Yes, but who is he?" They saw a tall black fellow with curly hair looks similar to crow's nest.

"That is lady's boyfriend."

"What?" All gave a gazed look towards Suju but got surprised to see a celebration being carried even in a remorseful day. Let people brand the incident in their own versions, but they are hardly bothered. Optimist can take their call and pessimists are open for their views. But one thing they vow is to run the celebration show.

Suju passed on a wink to the musician who asked the ladies for a dance. And hence Sibangini went to the dance floor with the strangers. Suju joined them leaving Srijesh and Ritee in their own company and their own space of comfort.

"Thanks for bringing us to this place Srijesh." And he heard his name being first time spelled by Ritee. It touched him to an extent of bringing a lean excitement.

"Now Sibangini almost reached her actual self. Malleable like a typical child, you bring her a chocolate and she will wipe her tears confronting every hostile situation. That is how she is," Ritee muttered her words.

"And you Ritee?"

"Me!" Ritee dwindled.

"Yes. What about you?"

"You can read the palms. May be you can read my face too Mr. Magician." Ritee pasted a witty smile on her face along with discretion.

"Okay, then spare me if I am wrong. To me, you are a confident and independent girl. The grace in your eyes clearly tells your dreams and the solid capability to achieve it. You have everything in you but at the same time I see you hiding many things inside your eyes and never show the pain behind it."

Ritee got alloyed by these remarks. Srijesh is absolutely correct. But how can she tell that a person who is weak inside tends to show a fake mask of toughness outside? She is speculative to be the real Ritee in front of him. Perhaps for her, Srijesh is still a stranger and it is premature to believe him. The more she kept silence Srijesh's patience became more vulnerable.

And she replied, "You are not wrong in judging me Srijesh. But all I can say is that I belong to a lower middle class family, where people still believe girls should not be more educated than boys. Rather female literacy itself is taboo for them. Sometime I feel jealous of you people. You have got everything and above all you guys are living a real peaceful life."

"Okay. Even I don't disagree with you Ritee. Neither am I having any right to complain against what you said. But let me tell something about us. Here people are so ingenuous and selfless. They never feel to compete with one another and never try to make others unhappy. Apart from their basic needs, one will get umpteen amount of love to be in this society. You know Ritee, here people hardly bother of their extra income or competitive professional life. You never find a commercial space open in the late evening. They are always more involved to their personal lives and keep on making it more enjoyable till they are alive. Here every day is beautiful than yesterday and tomorrow is even more beautiful than today."

Ritee believed blindly because she wanted to believe whatever Srijesh told. She could approve all his statements after looking at the houses, streets, the beautiful Christmas trees and the mirthful folks of Goa. The music stopped in between and there came the time of announcing the winners' names. While everyone became anxious for the result, Sibangini openly started asking her wishes with folded hands. But that was not the day of Bengali girls as they lost it from few European tourists.

"Oh no." Sibangini crossed her legs on the chair with frustration and puffed a long breath. After cursing the European tourists for a while she raised the Mojito glass and quickly finished it, which made her to sneeze twice.

"Are you ok?" Ritee asked her.

"What this mojito is made of, can anyone answer me?" Sibangini asked in a sneezing voice.

"Lady, this is made of blueberry flavour with liquor poured in it. Isn't it tasty?" Suju remarked quickly.

"What. Oh my God. Oh my God. Give me some water." By telling so she quickly drunk the other glass which was looking similar to colourless water, but Suju realized that Sibangini actually consumed the neat vodka which he has ordered for himself.

"Ahh . . . still bitter taste, can anybody give me some water please?" Sibangini started screaming which made Srijesh to call for the waiter, "Hey waiters, a glass of water please."

"Kya chahiye saab (What do you want sir)?" The waiter can speak only Hindi.

"Phani, phani. Ek glass phani (a glass of water)." Suju replied in Hindi knowing he is talking to a Hindi boy.

Sibangini quickly consumed another glass but realized it is a height of atrocity. How come water can give this kind of awful taste?

"What is this?"

The waiter politely replied, "Sir order kiya aapne Feni." (You ordered Feni sir).

"Arey bugger, phani not Feni, leave it." Before Sibangini could become totally off balanced, Suju took her to Parker's

Homestay which allowed Srijesh and Ritee to spend some more time with each other.

After spending few more minutes in the club, they took the beachside road for a walk, which leads to Parker's Homestay. By that time it was a clear moonlight flashing under the sky. Unknown to their respective feelings they were comfortable in giving mellow smiles to each other. They wanted to speak more but quite afraid of the proximity of their respective destinations. The more they come closer, they feel reluctant to proceed faster.

"Why are you so quiet?" Srijesh asked as he wished to read Ritee's silence.

"I don't know what to say? This is the first time I am away from my place, my people, my family and I am walking with a guy in this time of evening."

Srijesh could not predict anything but realized Ritee could have left along with Sibangini if she has the discomfort to be with him. But she didn't. He wanted to ask if she has a boyfriend but the last sentence of Ritee unfolded the truth and it certainly reinforced his attraction for her. But is it a mere attraction? No, something else he believed.

"Ritee, can I ask you something?" He raised again a boyish question meant to provoke the girls to think about them till the final question being queried.

"Yeah, ask?"

"Nothing, let it be."

"Arey, ask me?"

"So you like Goa it seems."

"Hmm. This is not what you meant earlier, isn't it? But as you asked, I would like to tell that your Goa is truly enchanting and magical. I hope these words fall smaller in front of its beauty. This is something beyond my imagination or knowledge, whatever. And in your language it is 'HEAVEN ON EARTH', apart from Blueberry Mojito and girls."

Srijesh could not control to grin as he felt Ritee has bought their words.

"Okay, accepted. And . . . what about the people?"

Before Ritee could answer subconscious truth, she understood Srijesh's intention to know 'about the people'. In short, it was about him. While looking at each other they smiled a bit and Ritee pushed back her attention with reluctance.

"You know the irony. It was me among our troop was totally uninterested to come to Goa, but I do realize now. I was wrong."

"So, are you feeling lucky to be here?"

"Yeah, feeling lucky. But not much huh, else we would have won that lucky draw." Ritee spoke leaving a childlike desire on her face.

A stone's throw distance to Parker's Homestay, they both were little hesitant to say good bye. Their momentum decelerated and they felt getting imprisoned by that moment. Their feet shrugged and could not able to uproot. No power has ever made to pause the time for a while. It was impossible to pacify the heart in that turmoil, they realized.

"So, we reached your place," a disheartened Srijesh told Ritee.

Ritee stood for a while and started circling her toe finger to the earth. "Ok, bye then." She turned around and started walking into the guest house. Even if she wanted, she was scared of looking back at Srijesh. So far his eyes have completely failed to hide his emotions for Ritee but vehemently expecting a mere glance from her that time. Srijesh knew that Ritee's small look can make his night. And he called, "Ritee . . . ." His voice sounds crystal clear. Ritee turned back. Oh God, she looked beautiful as she raised her eyebrows. Srijesh took out the envelope from his side pocket and handed it over to Ritee. And for a while Ritee turned wordless by thinking of her own, "My God, when this guy saved some time to write a letter for me?"

"What is this?" She asked.

Alas, the lucky draw prizes. A couple entry pass to the Blue Lagoon. Ritee blushed at her foolishness that made her to think about a letter. She was clueless, "Was it foolishness or a wish?"

She could not begin her question as it was unbelievable that Srijesh got the couple pass. "But . . ."

"Don't ask anything Ritee. I know you might feel peculiar but I am . . . I would like to take you to Blue Lagoon, if . . . if you feel it is right. If not, I won't ask. It is perfectly all right. Bye . . . and . . . good night." Srijesh's voice was incoherent and his tone slithered. He offered a friendly handshake but his hand wavered. And his eyes became shameful. But what Ritee read was entire different and it was speaking the truth lies beneath. It was not of an opportunist. Rather it was selfless. Selfless to read her wish to go to a new place and selfless to show her a beautiful tomorrow. She knew it would be impossible to refuse him by looking at the same selfless eyes. It would be unfair. But Srijesh left and gave her a space to think. To think before taking a bold decision to go along with a stranger to a new place. Even to a majestic one. But is it worthwhile to believe him. She kept her eyes closed and concluded that Srijesh was no longer a stranger, was he? She wanted to believe him, she wanted to trust him.

She returned to her bedroom and saw Sibangini riding a peaceful sleep being drunk. Asshole girl. Unconsciously she has spread her legs wide open turning her red skinny underwear completely visible. She hugged Sibangini and placed her cheek on her neck affectionately. She realized she is behaving like typical Sibangini when she has fallen in love for the first time. Is it the symptom? She whistled into her ear and tried to irate her. Perhaps she wanted to create some silly reasons for smiling. Slowly she caressed her hair and started smiling for her self-worthless act. Whether she has gone mad? Why the feeling of sweet sixteen started curbing her now? She closed her eyes simultaneously while clenching her fist. But it seems she has almost forgotten to sleep.

And Srijesh . . . poor fellow found the blunder activity of star counting would be more convenient than sleeping during that night.

11

*I*t was a bright sunny day. Ritee got up from bed in the early morning and found what Srijesh has told is completely true. Here every day is more beautiful than yesterday. But amidst this great feeling, there rose a scope of squabble inside the guest house. A cat fight was about to begin between Sibangini and Swati, where one was burning of jealousy and the other was travelling in vanity.

"Oh, it was a great dinner Sibangini. Delicious cuisine of all varieties, perfectly made sweet dish and if you see their house, you are gonna die. You should have come and see." Swati seemed as if she has come back from King's dining yesterday.

"Really," Sibangini said followed by a deep stillness.

"Yes, Professor was not letting us go yaar. Anyways, there are few more customs pending before marriage. He has personally requested us to participate in all the events." And she showed an excessive feeling of smug.

"Wow. Great." Sibangini did not find interesting at all. And again she chose to be silent. But Ritee entering into the room presumed the scenario as the silence appeared before storm. Sibangini tried to digress from the topic but Swati's hangover was having a delayed ending.

"You know there is an interesting custom here. It is called Ross ceremony which is similar to we put turmeric to bride and groom in Bengali marriage. Like that. Ross followed by wedding and finally the reception. Three days of extravaganza is still there." Swati gave her commentary in a single speech and her excitement was clearly seen dancing on her face.

"Over."

"Yeah."

"No no, you may continue if still something is pending."

"Why you are telling like this?"

"No because you left one more custom. You people are invited in all the customs right, so you would have got invitation to his honeymoon as well. To clean up their room, to decorate their bed, spray some erotic perfume in pillow, arrange some flowers to shower on their bed sheet and finally wash their shit in the morning, why the hell you all go and enter his asshole." Sibangini's voice aggravated exponentially and her tone seemed vomiting the venom. Everybody got thrilled by her behaviour. Moreover by looking at her face which turned fiery red.

"Excuse me Sibangini, but why are you reacting this way?"

"What excuse. Excuse me my foot, aren't you seeing I am not bothered to listen to your fucking speech. Just go to hell."

"Hey, now you are crossing your limit Sibangini."

"Who is crossing the limit, me or you?"

"Oh, stop it you two." And finally Ritee could not control her sentiments and reacted as a commanding template. She took Sibangini out of this loathsome conversation and pulled her to the terrace. After sitting for an hour both were not able to exchange a single word with each other. Ritee was damn furious whereas Sibangini was getting pacified by her own effort of self-consolation.

"Leave it dear. Nobody can realize my pain. Anyways, you tell, how is Mr. Musician?" An optimist Sibangini switched her mood in a fraction of second like a Chameleon.

"I am not concerned to attend your stupid jokes Sibangini. You have to tell me the truth. It was you among all, were desperate to come to Goa. Is it for this?" And Ritee raised her index finger tensely to know the naked truth, Sibangini has veiled so far.

Gasping a long breath Sibangini responded genuinely after wiping the last drop of tear, "Ok tell me, what you want to know?"

"The Truth." Ritee didn't tell any more words to intrigue as her silent face was demanding all answers from Sibangini.

"Fine. But you have to promise me Ritee; whatever I say . . . should not leak out from this room."

"You don't trust me Sibangini?"

"I do my dear. That's why I am revealing. You all know, I was in love with Prof. Ignesh. But nobody knows the complete story. It was supported equally by him."

"What are you saying Sibangini?" Ritee asked.

"Believe me dear, it is true. For me it is love, but for him it was all greed. It was the greed . . . to come closer to me and . . . and take whatever a man can take from a woman."

Ritee got completely frozen by her answer, knowing Sibangini never tells her a lie. And the truth came as a shockwave of life. She could not stop thinking if Sibangini has lost her rawness to Prof. Ignesh and she probed further, "Did you . . . did you sleep with him?"

Sibangini took her time but troubled her tongue by saying, "No dear, but believe me, we were so close . . . so close to each other and I was every day standing on the edge to submit myself. I was meeting him all the nights in his house without you people knowledge. We have madly kissed each other; we have touched each other everywhere and every time I managed to calm him down at that final moment. But one day . . . when I reacted strongly to his attempt, he stopped talking to me."

And she succumbed to weep once again.

"Baby, please, please don't. You have done no wrong."

"No I should have. I should have done wrong. I wish I would have got laid off with him and that could have ended his feelings stronger for me. That could have saved me . . . from his betrayal and I repent now and will be throughout my life." Ritee saw the blind possessiveness while listening to her carefully.

"Sibangini, look at me. Have you got blown out of your mind? What you are saying dear? How stupid you are. All the time I thought it's an attraction from your side which he never wanted to term as love. And you stupid girl, you believed his lust for you is his love, how could you dear?"

"It is the same way you feel Srijesh's love for you a mere attraction dear. The same way." Sibangini's words conserved Ritee's silence for a long time.

"Shut up . . . that is not true at all."

"Huh . . . it is. Don't question my experience Ritee. I have seen his eyes filled with lots of affection for you. I have seen him patiently looking at you going even though he knows, you won't turn back. And above all, he cares for you enormously. This is nothing but love for you my dear. I know how much it hurts if someone breaks your heart, but believe me it sends you heaven if somebody loves you unconditionally."

Ritee could not proceed for a word, but Sibangini's frustrating words sounded motivating to her that time.

"Sibangini, even I haven't told you one thing. Srijesh has asked me for an evening today."

"What . . . about the plan to visit Blue Lagoon resort?"

"How do you know?"

"I have already seen the passes in your carry bag?"

And Ritee raised her eyebrows, "You."

"So?"

"So what?"

"Arey, I am asking, what is your plan?"

"What plan, nothing?" Ritee curved her face to avoid Sibangini's naughty eye contact.

"Aha, then show me your face, show me your face Baby," Sibangini repeatedly cajoled by looking at her face that started melting with rosiness.

"Ouch." Sibangini poked Ritee's butt to bring her into ideal self from her bridal response.

"So tell me? What have you decided?"

"Still undecided," Ritee replied.

"What have we decided in the journey . . . that we will live to our fullest? And when you are getting an opportunity, why are you denying that my dear? It is not fair."

"But . . ."

"No but, you need to move only your butt." Sibangini knows in this scenario Ritee needs some fire behind, which will blaze her to show the magic of closeness of a guy and to fall in love. And she acted like a catalyst.

"If you were in my place, what you would have done?" Ritee asked.

"I am not a twit like you to refuse the proposal and especially if somebody else is sponsoring."

"You jerk." And they both smiled.

"No seriously, I would have said yes. What will happen in the future, nobody knows. Look Ritee, we both belong to the places where we can't pursue our dreams, neither our families are financially stronger. May be in future we both will be serving our in-laws like typical housewives. So let's stand by to these few days of Goa. And go . . . just step on to relish it." Sibangini's words seemed exceedingly provoking. Sibangini was never her idol neither Ritee was her follower at any point of time. But this time she wanted to believe her. She wanted to follow her and decide beyond what her mind recommends. But if she had listened to her heart, she would have known that has already given the approval. No turning back approval for her.

But among these excitements a meagre obstacle still exists. Sibangini has messed up with Swati and as a result Swati was in no purpose to go for Professor's Ross ceremony. Be it at the cost of crushing poor Chaterjee's heart. Only Sibangini can repair the situation and she did the same exactly so that her dear friend Ritee can go for a memorable date. The task was not so difficult and was resolved in the afternoon as girls accompanied Chaterjee to the function.

"How did you make it?"

"Anything for you Babe," Sibangini replied like a protective boyfriend to Ritee. She hugged her like a child and sneered.

No days were as much longer as today. The longings for meeting was making Ritee's wait even more delightful and bringing a newly bride's nervousness. It was impossible to count the heartbeat then, which was racing beyond her controller. Sibangini acted like a pacemaker to Ritee and helped her getting ready for the date. Most importantly she was helping her to look more beautiful than ever. Before Ritee contemplated her image in the mirror, the calling bell rang exactly at 4pm.

"I think he has come." An exulted Sibangini thought to open the door before Ritee held her hand to pause for a moment.

"Oh my God," Ritee said placing her right plam on her chest. She felt losing all her strength that time. Sibangini slowly lifted Ritee's palm from her hand and approached towards the door. She opened it quickly disallowing Srijesh to trouble for his second bell.

"Hello Mr. Musician."

Looking at Sibangini he greeted, "Hi, I am not surprised at all."

"But I am. You are late. Everybody has left for the function including Ritee."

"Really, very funny."

"Don't worry hero, there she is." Sibangini decided not to produce any more jolt for the lovers. Srijesh turned around towards the stair and looked at Ritee who lifted her eyelid to look at him in reply. It was not new to his eye that she looks beautiful, but that day she bought him completely. He escorted her to his vehicle parked outside and opened the front door. They left for Blue Lagoon. Not to forget, it was located in Anjuna Beach, the synonym of celebration in Goa.

They have eased with their exchange of words till yesterday like friends. But today's scenario was little different. Thousand words of Srijesh were searching for their right path to get translated into his voice, whereas Ritee on the other hand was behaving like a reticent girl. Perhaps she was still undecided whether she has taken the right decision to come along with him. Keeping reluctance, she was looking out of the glass door when Srijesh slowly put on the power window button. A gentle wind dishevelled her for a while. Today her hair is unclogged and it got misaligned completely till she placed her hand to adjust it. She has almost achieved it except a strand of hair which got tangled to the black mascara and partially clung to the red silky lipstick on her lower lips. In the crux of settling her hair, she managed to look at Srijesh who posed a greeting smile once again.

"Thanks for coming Ritee."

Ritee smiled, "Ah, what time we shall reach there?" She asked to avoid the engaging words from Srijesh.

"I told thanks for coming," Srijesh recapped and Ritee could not do much than reserving the silky smile of her lips.

They passed by the city and gradually ran through the marine drive. For Srijesh, more than the joy of ride, it was the presence of Ritee. They entered the Blue Lagoon resort and got a warm welcome from the staffs as well as the ambiance. The celebration was about to begin. During the entire ride Srijesh had kept a surprise present for Ritee. But he knew, it was not the day to hide, it was the day to be you and listen to the heart.

"Ritee, if you don't mind, I have got something for you." By saying it so, while walking on the lobby, he handed over the parcel to Ritee.

"But how can I?"

"This is not a gift Ritee. At least take it for today. And there is my small wish attached to it."

"What?" Ritee blushed.

"I want you to look more beautiful than anybody else present in this function. I just want you look what you deserve Ritee." Srijesh actively knows how to impress the girl. Those words made Ritee lost for a while and she went to the change room. In a cautiously wrapped parcel, she found a black sumptuous gown with white colour stones and embroidery work attached to it. But the true surprise was a creamy pearl necklace which she realized as the best choice of Srijesh. She took her usual time to get ready and came out. She hardly saw her face in the mirror in between the curiosity to show it to Srijesh. And what Srijesh saw today completely hypnotized him. He knew it was going to be recalled for lifetime in his mind. She looks ravishing. More than anybody and more than what he has imagined. There were no words to describe. She looks elegant, she looks stunning and Srijesh wanted to praise her not with a desire of flattering but to tell the truth. And more over anything, today she is looking like a gorgeous lady who can attract any handsome man present in the function. A perfectly fit black gown whose bottom was partially falling at her knee height making her slim fair legs beautifully visible on her stiletto and the top part was allowing for an ultra-shine look of her neck by exposing the cleavage up to a small extent. The heart shaped face doubled the beauty blending with creamy pearl necklace. Srijesh swallowed hard as he got completely sold by the charismatic beauty of this lady called Ritee. Somehow Ritee knew that she is looking different the way Srijesh looked at her. She felt engrossed and was thirsting for his appreciation which drew her to ask, "How am I looking?"

"Shhhh. You don't need any appreciation Ritee. You will soon come to know the answer. Rather I feel, you need protection. So just hold on my hand."

Ritee glowed to those words and said, "Aha, nice way to flirt."

"Just kidding, let's go inside." Srijesh took Ritee along with him to the main event. She has never been to this kind of places before. But today she looks like a tasty eye candy and she gradually started receiving attention from most of the attendants. What Srijesh told, that came like a surprise truth to her. She needs protection.

"I told you," Srijesh said the moment he realized Ritee hold his hand. Be it subliminally but she was not taking those out. She feels protective. She couldn't even imagine being like this in her place, wearing a sexy gown, dating a guy in this luxury resort and enjoying the moments. She felt there is no wrong in it. Who can see her? She posed a 'WHO CARES' attitude. She was not with them who try to belittle her. Truly, she was a free bird that time. And the free bird desired to live every second of that evening.

Srijesh offered a chair to Ritee like a gentleman and sat beside her after bringing two soft drinks. It was the time of Goan trance music to get rejuvenated. It was enough to take them out of their seat to the spacious stage. If not, the music host does the rest. "Everybody on the stage please." That very moment Ritee realized the place was full of couples when all together joined the stage. Before Ritee could think about some excuses Srijesh offered his hand and did not allow her to refuse for a dance. He took her hand and gently pulled her towards the stage. Ritee didn't want to miss the feel of a princess the way Srijesh carried her. The trance bounced back inviting everyone to bother their feet and tap harder. The crowd got misaligned resulting Ritee to lose Srijesh's hand and got missed somewhere. Lights got dimmed and became more romantic. Couples got fused together in each other's arms when trance shifted to soft music. Her eyes started searching for the known face of Srijesh and suddenly few fingers tapped her shoulder. She looked back and took a sigh of relief causing her eyes closed. And when she opened it, she realized the spaces between her fingers were filled as Srijesh held her hand softly. She felt his touch magical while keeping the eyes closed. They went cosy for a long time and whispered to each other.

"Ritee, let me tell you the truth. You are looking so beautiful." Ritee shied at Srijesh's convincing look which weighs more than these words.

"Shall I ask you one thing?"

"Yeah."

"I am little surprised. How come you know this gown will fit me?"

"Means."

"Means, how come you know my . . . my . . ."

"What, your figure size."

"You . . ." Ritee lifted her eyes and blushed for a moment. Gazing each other, they felt like knowing each other for a long time. The buzz of the seashore became audible when music slowed down. Ritee didn't expect the sea to be situated so nearer to this beautiful resort. She insisted Srijesh to take her near to the sea. Perhaps she felt they have come closer on the dance floor and it will be too late if she doesn't distract him now. They withdrew their cosiness and moved near to sea. And then what Ritee saw was unbelievable. To her surprise, it was jam-packed surpassing the crowd inside the resort.

"Wow." She got completely thrilled by this astonishing view of the sea water. Whether a beach could be more beautiful than this? It is not new to her. Of course she has viewed it near to her native. But could it be utilized the way this one is, unimaginable? This place looks like an island out of any connection from the world. Everybody was in their own tune and in the company of their very own people.

"Can I ask you one more thing Srijesh, please don't take me wrong?"

"Why, what happened?"

"I wonder what you might be thinking about me. I am alone here roaming with someone whom I hardly know for few days."

"This will be applicable to me as well Ritee. I also know hardly about you but I am feeling glad to be with you."

"But your situation is different?"

"And why is it so?"

"Because you are a guy and . . . I am a girl."

"So what, I don't see any problem."

"As a guy, it might be very common for you Srijesh. May be your place, your society allow you to be the way you decide. You would be roaming along with your friends without any restrictions; you might be dating a girl . . . ?" Before Ritee could express few more words, Srijesh hush her by placing his finger on her lips. He looked distinctly into her eyes and said, "I don't have a girlfriend Ritee."

This sentence touched Ritee and now she can take Srijesh into confidence. A strong flow of sea wave drenched them partially. Srijesh took a bit of sand and touched Ritee's cheek to bring her angelic smile back.

Generally girls don't say this paradoxical statement. But Ritee sounded like a child when she told, "Srijesh, now I am feeling hungry." And Srijesh was touched by her ingeniousness. Gourmet dinner was being served in the rooftop restaurant. Few perfectly cooked nicely smelled Western food which could make everyone to get salivated. Waiter served the items one by one but it seemed a mammoth task for Ritee to taste it with the help of fork and knife. Srijesh tried his best to guide her but the difficulty level was already at a par of rocket science for Ritee. And so did her comfort level which deteriorated in front of the cosmopolitan guests.

"Ritee, have you heard about moon light dinner?"

"No, I have heard only about candle light dinner," Ritee replied that made Srijesh to smile a bit at her innocence. He packed as much dry items as possible inside his guitar bag without anybody's notice. There was no other option but to flee from this strained situation, but it was tough to surpass the security gate. Srijesh insisted Ritee to hold his forearms the way Western couple does. They both became sure to divert the attention of the guard, if they look like genuine couple. The moment they came out of the main gate Srijesh switched on the vehicle and rolled it with full speed till they reached one secluded place. They madly laughed what they were regulating for the entire ride.

"Oh my God, it was crazy," Ritee took a long breath and said while placing her hands on the chest.

"Ok, ok, let's have dinner," Srijesh too told in his tiresome voice.

"But how?"

Srijesh realized it is not the full moon night and he lighted few wood pieces in supplement. No dinner is complete without drinks which he has carried with him. But it was a fruit beer bottle containing zero per cent alcohol.

"Dinner is ready."

Ritee was looking patiently at the act done by Srijesh. Though it was madness but she got impressed by this effort. They had the so called moonlight dinner in absence of required tools. They had paper box instead of plates, moonlight instead of candle light. So foolish yet so romantic as they had an innocent sky with some twinkling stars above them watching this crazy couple on earth.

"So this is your guitar huh." Ritee took the guitar and started wiping the strings.

"Wow Madonna, you look like a rock star."

"I will play a song now."

"All yours."

Ritee twisted the guitar string which gave the ugliest sound this guitar has ever produced.

"Wow." Srijesh clapped.

"Ha ha ha, I know it is irritating. It will suit you only."

"Wait. I will teach you." Srijesh came behind and surrounded Ritee's hand to touch the strings once again. Ritee felt like being clutched inside Srijesh's body. It was certainly very different than the touch they had while dancing. It is not the crowded place like the resort. They both could feel the loneliness and Srijesh was busy in demonstrating the magic of guitar. By realizing the equal effort was not being made by Ritee, he looked into her eyes. And this time he saw something different. He saw what he has wished to see in her eyes before. Ritee didn't divert her attention, neither had she looked intimidated. But this time she closed her eyes allowing Srijesh to take the decision. He could listen to her breath which made him to swallow harder. Is she ready for a kiss or is it early to think about. He was still undecided by fighting with his own gullible thoughts.

"Please let me go Srijesh," Ritee said and Srijesh felt like missing the golden opportunity.

He slowly took off his hands which made his lovely guitar fell down on the sand. Ritee took few steps forward but did not dare to look back at Srijesh. She crossed her palms on her shoulder to quench the mild cold and Srijesh covered her by his jacket. He made her turn around and created little strength to propose.

"Ritee, for me this is the first time and maybe I sound little weird but I would like to tell you something."

"Let's go Srijesh."

"I don't know how will you take it?"

"Let's go, please."

"But I really have to say this . . ."

"Please let me go Srijesh."

"I have started liking you Ritee."

Ritee paused for a while and spoke when her mind took over the heart, "Why Srijesh? We hardly know each other."

"What do you expect Ritee? Do I have to know you, examine you before falling in love with you? I am not so selfish to judge you first and then express my feelings."

"Exactly, you can't judge me. Because you don't know me Srijesh. We are from different place, different caste and most importantly from different religion. There cannot be any match between us. I have already told about the place, the society where I do belong to. I am not blessed like you Srijesh. So I can't."

"You can't or you don't Ritee," Srijesh asked firmly.

"Whatever, will you please drop me to the guest house?"

Srijesh somehow controlled his outrage against Ritee's stringent words. He dropped her to Parker's Homestay without speaking anything during the drive. And finally before leaving he could not halt his mouth and said, "I will wait for your answer Ritee."

For the first time Ritee felt hurt while watching Srijesh leaving. She started feeling like he will not come here again. Oh God, what has she done? The day has been the best day of her life if she erases some portion of it when she broke Srijesh's heart. She never wanted to, but she is not ready yet. She can't rewind the time else she would have given a different acceptance to his proposal. Before Ritee could travel again to her unresolved thoughts, she heard a narrow voice under the recognition.

"Ritee, hey . . . Ritee." The voice was coming behind the bush and it was of Sibangini's.

"Hey, what are you doing here?" Ritee asked her surprisingly.

"Just forget about me. What were you doing till now? You know the guys have come to our guest house and this time including Parthoda. He is asking about you," Sibangini said furiously this time.

"What did you tell then?" Ritee asked in a scary tone.

"I told you have gone for an evening walk. Let's go now. But my dear what . . . have . . . you . . . worn . . . ? It is certainly not the evening walk clothes. My God, where did you get it?" Sibangini reacted like she just saw the eighth wonder of the world. But the truth was she had actually not seen this kind of gown before.

"Remove it," Sibangini told at once.

"What?"

"I mean change . . . change it. Where is your dress dear, please change it, else we will get screwed up?"

"Oh no. I left inside Srijesh's car. What to do," Ritee replied and started biting nail.

"Excellent. You left in Srijesh's car. Now what to do? They will ask so many things . . . one minute; hang on . . . by the way . . . why you change the dress. Tell me the truth, what made you to undress inside the car huh?" Sibangini asked by flaunting her ravening eyes.

"Oh stop it. You dirty creature. You better think how to survive from this situation?" Ritee asked in a tensed voice.

"They have already seen me, but if they don't meet you now, it will be tragic." Sibangini pulled her inside the bush and started removing her skirt.

"What are you doing?"

"Just do as I say. You also remove your dress."

"Have you gone mad?"

"Arey, let's exchange it for time being my dear and I will stay here for a while till you come back." While Ritee wore Sibangini's dress for the time being, Sibangini just held the gown to hide her breasts and sat inside the bush.

"I will come back soon."

"You have to; else you will find me being raped here."

Ritee could not control laughing and rushed inside the guest house.

"Namaskar dada."

"Hello ma Ritee. How are you? You came alone and now where is that stupid girl Sibangini?" Parthoda asked.

"Dada, she is speaking to the house owner."

"Very good. You girls became very smart in Goa huh. One is going for evening walk and other is speaking to the foreigners. Quite impressive huh." Parthoda doesn't know that girls are master in bluff. And poor fellow was trying to appreciate them.

"Ok, so you all had dinner?"

"Yes dada," all replied typically the way children respond to the head of the family.

"Good, now I feel relaxed. Chaterjee, shall we make a move now?"

They both left and Ritee took a heave of relief. But she had got one more job to do and that was to rescue semi-nude

Sibangini. She ran to that place but got shocked by seeing Parthoda pissing near to the bush where Sibangini had apparently hidden herself. "Oh my God, no more exploit please," she started praying. After few minutes Chaterjee and Parthoda left the campus permanently while Ritee along with Sibangini came down to their bed room. She could not control her laughter leaving Sibangini embarrassed like anything. But jolly good girl even now accompanied her in smiling and said, "Thank God, I was about to take bathe in Parthoda's hand pump. Oh, narrow escape, really."

The dilemma in Ritee's mind still went on. She was not able to forget the moments spent with Srijesh and moreover his greedy face. It was enough to keep her wakeful that night.

12

$\mathcal{R}$itee came to know about morning when her dreams got crushed. She has not spent a sound sleep and woken up several times during the night. She came out of the room and saw the clear sky looked beaming with the sun shine. It made her feel the new beginning of her love life.

She got despairingly muddled by looking at Sibangini who glared at her while setting the bed sheet.

"What?" And Ritee gave a nasty look too.

"What do you think? Whatever you are doing is right?"

"What? What am I doing?"

"Huh, as if I don't know anything. You are a novice in this field my dear, I have got lot more experience than you," Sibangini told by taking a pride in her voice and was in a mood to intrigue Ritee's feeling for Srijesh.

"How come you know?"

"You grudged his name at least four or five times in your sex dreams. Srijesh . . . Srijesh . . . ohh Srijesh . . . ohh Srijesh," Sibangini mimicked.

"Really, what nonsense. I don't think so."

"Huh, tell me seriously, what have you decided for Srijesh?"

"Nothing. I want to forget him and about yesterday completely," Ritee replied.

"You are a fool."

"Just think of it by keeping yourself in my place Sibangini."

"Exactly, I would have never done that."

"That is why you are facing the consequence. You do realize. Don't you?" Ritee counter attacked Sibangini.

"Huh, you will also face the same dear. Just wait and watch. We both have done the same errors. You know what, I chose a wrong person unknowingly and you are not choosing the right person knowingly. Anyways, you are the best judge of your own life. I won't tell anything. Enjoy." Sibangini's words started piercing Ritee and turned her even more puzzled this time.

Chotu delivers them breakfast early morning and that day it was 8 am in the watch. Usually girls take the parcel and send him off from the door itself. But today he got astounded by seeing the warm welcome extended to him by Sibangini. She started chatting with Ritee for a long time in her own language unknown to the fact that Chotu can actually make out. He came to know they are talking about Srijesh and he decided to put some oil on the fire, if they ask him anything about Srijesh. What he presumed, it happened. They discussed some mundane topics and finally ended up what they intent to know.

"How is Mr. Musician by the way?" Sibangini asked in a very casual way so that Chotu can't pretend anything.

"Yeah, he is fine," Chotu answered.

"Really, is he fine?" Ritee's feminine ego spoke for herself as she was expecting a heartbroken story of last night.

Chotu never hesitates to pronounce Ritee as 'Didi' knowing she is his Srijesh Bhaiya's love interest. And finally he spoke after looking here and there for a minute.

"Didi, he has gone out of his mind. For the first time in life I saw him drinking last night. We felt miserable for him and asked for the reason but he didn't disclose anything. He just wanted to show us that only diamond can cut the diamond and he continued drinking Rum. You know Rum, which can take life too. My Srijesh Bhaiya is the most innocent person in the world and he has never done anything wrong to anybody. I don't know why God is giving him so much pain." Chotu acted like he was in an inch distance to be collapsed. Girls accepted his speech being unknown to the power of overacting skill pursued by him. Girls again discussed something but Chotu realized they actually wanted to go to Srijesh's house. Chotu can dream about the brutal situation if girls visit their house. He can't even imagine what the situation will be if they see hundreds of liquor bottles along with thousands of used condom packets thrown in their back gate area. Courtesy to the all-time fucker Suju.

"Nooooooo." An unconscious reply coughed up from Chotu's mouth as he screamed. Ritee and Sibangini looked at him with shock and awe, "What happened?"

"No, you should not go there right now Didi."

"Where? When we told we want to go somewhere?"

Chotu gulped and said, "I just guessed you want to meet Srijesh Bhaiya as you asked about him."

"So, why are we banned to go to his house?" Sibangini asked.

"Because, because . . . he is not there right now. He has gone to the hotel and will follow straight to Prof. Fernandes marriage afterwards." Chotu marginally escaped from this tragedy and thought to leave from there before Sibangini interrupted him once again, "Chotu, can you do us a favour. Can you inform your Srijesh Bhaiya to meet us once during marriage time? May be near to the church area?"

Chotu nodded his head and sprinted to Srijesh. He told him about the whole incident and about their meeting plan. Srijesh's confidence got thrived and numbers of thoughts started jogging inside his mind. The curiosity heightened and his patience stood in a long queue to wait for the afternoon. Knowing marriage ceremony is at 3 o' clock, he decided to reach before time.

13

$\mathcal{I}$t was the marriage date. Girls know the D day is here for which they have come a long way to Goa. They wanted to look best ever but knew it won't be possible without wearing traditional Bengali Sari. Girls consumed more time than required but reached on time to church where the marriage ceremony was being held. Sibangini and Ritee waited in front of the church gate after sending others inside. After few minutes of wait Chotu came towards them and showed his Srijesh Bhaiya standing way out of the compound facing the seashore. Sibangini patted Chotu's shoulder and took him inside the church. Now Ritee knows, she has to proceed alone to meet Srijesh and express herself. By leaning on a coconut tree Srijesh saw Ritee coming fearlessly. Day by day Ritee seems more beautiful to him. He has never thought Ritee appearing in front of him all alone and accepts his proposal. But even this time his expectations splintered when Ritee started speaking baseless which Srijesh was least fascinated to give attention.

"Srijesh, I know how you feel for me. But believe me, I am helpless. Look, I am the eldest child in my family. My father has seen few dreams for me. He wants me to be a responsible part of our family. He feels, someday I will become his supportive hand. I can't leave them neither they will leave me even after my marriage. So just throw me out of your mind Srijesh. Just forget me." Ritee looked entirely confused and Srijesh smiled by thinking what Suju has told him once. "Girls behave very confused while they fall in love."

"Srijesh, I know you must be thinking what this stupid girl is talking all about. But believe me. The truth is that I have never come across this kind of situation before." Ritee again tried to defend herself. Srijesh thought of himself, "What Ritee meant finally. What she is trying to justify? Is she trying to say that she is first time in love?" And finally Ritee said which is universally loathed by most of the guys when a girl replies. "You must have come across many girls and may be the feeling for me will be a mere infatuation of yours. So the solution is LET'S BE FRIENDS. JUST FRIENDS."

Srijesh smiled and said, "So for this you have called me. You don't have to say all this Ritee, I respect your feelings. Come, I will show you the auspicious marriage function in presence of God." He took her inside the church without fading his ray of hopes. Because Ritee, so far, has not told that she doesn't like him. May be she has not accepted his proposal but she has not refused it either.

They entered the church and moved to the corner most places. It was a pin drop silence amidst hundreds of attendants. A soothing lullaby started when the bride entered the place. Her ethereal beauty was encompassed by stars spotted white bridal veil. The Priest invited the bride and groom to the prayer stage and finally instructed to abide the solemn pledge.

At this time in presence of Lord Jesus, I invite both of you to face each other.

"Ignesh, will you take Silviya to be your wife, your partner and true love in your life? Will you cherish her friendship and love her forever? Will you trust and respect her? Will you laugh and cry with her? Will you be faithful to her in bad and good times, in sickness and in health as long as you both shall live?"

"I do."

Silviya, will you take Ignesh to be your husband, your partner and true love in your life? Will you cherish his friendship and love him forever? Will you trust and respect him? Will you laugh and cry with him? Will you be faithful to him in bad and good times, in sickness and in health as long as you both shall live?"

"I do."

"Now I pronounce you husband and wife. May God bless you."

People started praying for the newlywed couple. Srijesh hold Ritee's hand and helped her to say, "Amen." For a thin moment they both dreamt of being on the stage and finally

Srijesh proposed after taking her hands close to his heart, "Ritee, I am not a daring person to tell a lie in front of almighty God. And hence I say . . . I love you, I love you a lot."

Ritee stood inanimately for a while. She looked Srijesh invigoratingly before the crowd got untied. She has started loving Goa from day one. She repents herself as why she is not among one of them here. Every step she puts forward she gets replenished by the joy of this place, the marriage, the customs and above all the joy of being with Srijesh. She wanted to spend some more time with him but the present circumstance didn't allow her. They both were among all other guests in the marriage. Before she could answer anything, her friends took her along with them to Prof. Ignesh's house where marriage reception was being organized in a lavish manner. Ritee left by keeping a prayer in her mind to meet Srijesh in the marriage reception.

The evening truly belonged to Fernandes family who has thrown an unforgettable bash. Guests have been cheering for the celebration. However, being separated from the crowd Ritee was curiously waiting for Srijesh and Sibangini was accompanying her for namesake but was unknown to the forthcoming awkward moments. Prof. Ignesh came near to the Bengali esteemed guests and started introducing them to his bride. The heavenly beauty with power packed attitude of the bride started slicing everybody's confidence and Sibangini felt very small in front of her. She along with Ritee decided to leave the place but changed their decision after seeing Srijesh coming to the party. Today also he came like a saviour. They moved to the corner place and talked for a long time like known friends. Sibangini gave both of them umpteen spaces to come closer. She was again acting like a catalyst for the future bonding to happen between Srijesh and Ritee. They both looked perfectly made for each other. Ritee seemed to accept his proposal anytime. In between they summoned for dinner followed by some drinks. They both looked devastated as time flied on a faster rate. They spent a quality time together and Ritee felt being on the verge to take a decision in favour of Srijesh. But she could not.

14

It was December 30th and was the penultimate day of the climax of their journey. Parthoda had booked the ticket of 31st December by expecting very limited numbers of people travel on the last day of the year. It happened to be true as they got confirmed rail ticket to Howrah.

Girls arranged their luggage knowing they might not get sufficient time for doing this work today evening. They have to be present for a small party organized by Prof. Ignesh, which is bestowed to the friends. Exclusively for friends and no elders were invited. Sibangini and Ritee were no different either but they were busy in realizing the emptiness beleaguered them. One lost her past and other is going to lose her future during the same time while leaving from Goa. By that time Sibangini had completely vacuumed the love portion from her mind, but she was very much aware of her friend Ritee who was falling for Srijesh. There are some people on earth who never hesitate to help others even though they are dipping into their own pain of ocean like an iceberg. Sibangini was one that type of character who is still impatient in curbing Ritee's heart to speak truth and facilitates her to express the hidden love for Srijesh.

"So, last day huh?" Sibangini put an exclamation.

"I know it. Anyways, thanks for reminding," Ritee said filled with an irritation in her voice.

"Yeah, yeah, But you don't see what I can. Back to Kolkata, same college, same old roads, a monotonous life. You know, some people think of achieving their self-importance by constantly smothering their own love at the cost of their superego. Isn't it?" Sibangini irked with her never-ending philosophical words.

"Why are you playing with your words Sibangini? Please be open. I know what you want to say. For you it is easier to love someone and forget after some point of time. Isn't it? But the same is not valid for me Sibangini. You want to know how I feel about Srijesh. How I react when he expects me to turn back and how I think about him during whole night? I know there are cobwebs of questions loaded inside your mind. And your answer to all these questions is yes. Yes Sibangini. I do love him. I am mad for his love, his care and respect for me. When he looks at me I want to be the most beautiful girl in the world. The way he cares for me I feel to be with him all the time. And the way he loves me I want to submit my entire life to him. But I can't. You know why, I live in the same barbarian society where you do. He is not of our religion and I can't honour my commitment if I accept his love. I am not able to see any future with him Sibangini. I know, last few days were the best days of my life but I just want to forget those as a sweet memory. Help me in doing this and please . . . please don't add anymore miseries in my life. Please help me," Ritee said equipped with a stream of tear in her eyes.

Sibangini never believed a strong girl like Ritee could ever melt like this. She tried to reassure her being a faithful friend and decided not to sprinkle salt on her burn. Ritee felt like conveying a farewell to the journey. She even decided not to meet Srijesh till they leave Goa. They didn't welcome Chotu unlike yesterday. They did not come out when Srijesh tried to meet them and finally they decided to skip the evening party expecting Srijesh to be present there.

Ritee felt choked every moment the day passed by. She closes her eyes and tries to think about her own place, own people but ends up seeing Srijesh. It is not possible. Mere six days can't bring so close to a person. How he has become so own to her. Why she is not able to stop her mind running close to Srijesh. "My God, give me strength." Is it because she is leaving tomorrow and has no hope left to meet Srijesh again. She felt commiserated on her haplessness. Why she has succumbed to her weakness. "Oh God, please omit the past few days of my life and throw me somewhere in the gullies of Kolkata," she started praying.

It was late evening when everybody were enjoying Prof. Ignesh's party, Sibangini heard her friend Ritee was weeping from the other corner of the house.

"Hey, Baby what happened?" She felt the tremor of her body when she embraced her.

"Sibangini, I need to see him once. Just once. I will see him from a distance and come back. I swear."

Sibangini realized and smiled secretly. She knew this situation would come. Her Darling Ritee has fallen in love. She praised her own experience as her prediction came true. And like a loyalist she took her to the evening party which was not far from their residence. It was organized in an open air beach side restaurant led by newly married couple Mr. and Ms. Ignesh Fernandes. Ritee saw Srijesh seized by many of his friends but he managed to swing his hand after seeing her entering the banquet. Ritee stared at Srijesh by the help of her moist eyes and walked past the restaurant to a lonely place off seashore. Srijesh followed her alone and asked while standing behind, "Hey Ritee, what happened. Why are you not joining others? Come, you will have fun." He behaved just like a casual friend. How rude?

"Fun, huh! Life is all about making fun for you right. Stop behaving like a caring friend. Where have you flushed this decent behaviour Mr. Srijesh when you proposed me, huh? Once I instructed you to be my friend, you started copying that. How soon can you switch your mood, isn't it? Is that your love lasts for? You all guys are same. If one girl accepts your proposal, it is ok. If not, let's try for some other girls. Is that your love means to you?"

Srijesh looked blank, complete blank clouded on his face. In one spin he felt like Ritee has lost her consciousness and in other he felt like Ritee's resentment was speaking for her. He wanted to look at Ritee's face which has gathered enough strength to rebuke him, but her hair has almost covered it as that day wind was irresistible. He came closer and gained strength as Ritee did not step back; he lifted her hair out of her face and mustered up courage as Ritee did not shut her eyelid. But he saw her face crimsoned and hands began to shake when he hold her palm. And he expressed his muffled desire with a lusty touch on her lips which his words were unable to describe so far. He kissed her amorously as they both closed their eyes. And for the first time they felt the succulent taste of each other.

"This is not right Srijesh." Ritee pushed him and said in a husky voice. Srijesh tried to fetch her hand before she moved few steps farther.

"Why Ritee? You still disbelieve my love for you."

"Yes." Ritee's tonality didn't change at all.

"Then why have you come here Ritee?"

"Just to tell you that we are leaving tomorrow," Ritee replied.

"Then look at me and say it Ritee. And say that you don't love me." Srijesh fetched her cheeks by his palms to catch her eye contact. Ritee felt helpless being submissive towards the deep drawn love along with the enduring passion inherited by Srijesh. A solitary tear trickled down from her eyes and its warmth made Srijesh to release her. She tried to leave the place and Srijesh furnished his last hope into few words.

"Ritee, I will wait for you here entire night. If you won't come, I will accept that I was wrong in recognizing your love."

Ritee did not stop.

How can she sleep that night being drowned into her thoughts? She remembered Srijesh's eyes replenished with overwhelming love and passion for her. She felt restless every second by thinking about the magnetic touch of Srijesh. She felt being crawled towards him. The exhilarating passion showed by Srijesh left her with two choices. First one is to forget the entire memories of last seven days like a fairy tale dream and the second is to go . . . go and meet him for one last time. And she chose the second one.

It was midnight when everybody was relishing in dreams; she took her scarf and jumped out of the compound. She broke every possible hindrance on her way. In self-contempt, she didn't even bother to inform Sibangini. She adjudicated to submit herself to Srijesh if he shows his endless patience to wait for her that night. If not, she will grant him as a normal acquaintance that she got infatuated once. She wished Srijesh would not have waited for her. But her diminished expectation came alive when she found Srijesh stood leaning on the rock. Srijesh could not trust his eyes as he saw Ritee right in front of him without any make up on her face. She has come with her bare feet. She was looking like an ordinary girl who has skipped her hunger to attract others. She looks tender and desired to feel the warmth of Srijesh. The quiver in her body died when she hugged him and posted a thirsty kiss on his lips. Srijesh embraced her in return and ingested her with countless kisses in her mouth. They both saw excessive flow of love in each other's eyes which started melting into a form of frantic desire in their bodies. Without caring each other's emotions they progressed farther and farther. They didn't stop being blessed with the absence of any living or non-living objects that could hinder their intimacy. The pleasure of love making surpassed the immaturity and pain of their bodies while getting fused together on the lap of the sand. They got blown away in each other's arms for a long time and grounded their exuberance when Srijesh climaxed his pleasure inside Ritee. But it was too late to protect her virginity.

After reaching the pinnacle of love making they both felt robbed off with their words. They spent few more minutes of speechlessness. Ritee felt shy of the awkward intimate positions shared with Srijesh few minutes back. She clothed herself standing behind the other side of the rock. Srijesh wanted to hug her; he wanted to kiss her forehead as a reward for accepting his love. He wanted to tell infinite times how much he loves her but could not say a word when he saw tears in Ritee's eyes. It was more of the guilt than the pain she bore while losing her tenderness. And Srijesh was having no answer to her furtive eyes.

It was 4 am in the watch and both were conscious enough to decide the leaving time for their respective places. Srijesh accompanied Ritee as he had to post her unscathed to Parker's Homestay without anybody's notice. He relaxed for a moment when Ritee entered the house safely and by the time he entered his, it was early morning. He didn't want to sleep as he promised Ritee to meet her in station. Ritee could not sleep either as she has not been able to come out of the horrific incident which she has never accepted to perform before marriage. How can she believe she lost her most precious part so easily, which she has been preserving for last nineteen years? Her effusive mind searched for a pen and paper and wrote a letter for Srijesh. She decided to handover it before leaving for Kolkata.

After conveying a final goodbye to Parker family, they left for station before one hour of schedule departure. This time Suju accompanied them. Last seven days were the most memorable days for all of them and they were carrying all the sweetest memories to their respective lives. Everybody had a nostalgic smile on their face except Ritee. Nobody knows how much they have gained from this journey but Ritee feels as if she has lost much more. The scenery of Goa, the trees, the sparkling sea water that has mesmerized her once, now looks dull and exhausted to her eyes.

Srijesh didn't know what made him to close his eyes but when he got up, he did not expect to sleep for such long hours. He had to meet Ritee who was leaving Goa permanently. He started his bike with optimum speed and raced towards the station as he was yearning for a glimpse of her.

Visitors thanked Suju for the courtesy he has extended to them and making their journey worthwhile. For the first time Suju got touched by his customers. The departure time came nearer but Ritee could not see Srijesh so far. Her hope got faded as the siren bell rang. Her notion of detesting the guys became stronger when she could not find Srijesh before time. But train left Vosco Station maintaining its accuracy.

Srijesh ran unceasingly towards the platform but it was too late. He could not forgive himself for not able to see Ritee's face for the last time. He felt like killing himself in madness. He knew this mistake will hunt him forever.

Ritee accepted the fact that she did the greatest sin of her life last night. She took out the letter furiously which she has written with utmost care and hope for Srijesh. She came out of her compartment and cried blatantly in presence of lot many travellers inside the train. She tore the letter in extreme anger where it was written:

Dear Srijesh,

A night comes in every girl's life where she has to submit herself to someone. But I never expected it to come in such a way for me. I wish, I could completely believe you but my nerves are still acting against me. You came in my life as a thunder and displaced me like a dry leaf of desert. Last night was a crime we have done. But it is always the weaker sex has to pay the price in our cynical society. And I know I have to pay for it. So I request you never ever try to contact me. If you have ever loved me, then I know you will allow me to forget these last seven days. Please keep my words. And in future if our path crosses then I will welcome the fact that God has written something for us.

And she had not written her name below.

15

It was almost a week of the New Year and Ritee had been rattling in her own thoughts from day one. Every time she was alone, she tried to be judicious and comparative to the last few days of her life. She realized life has become monotonous now. But she has enjoyed the monotony so far if she excludes her seven days spent in Goa. She was deeply sceptical about her near future due to that incident which disallowed her to come out of the trauma. She felt like she has killed her inner self. She felt small and degraded, whenever she looked her naked body in front of the mirror. She realized if she coerces her mind this way perhaps she will go mad after some point of time. She united her suppressed strengths and became transparent to Sibangini. Her only objective was to seek some consolation from her.

"What . . . ?" Sibangini reacted as if somebody hammered her head with an Iron rod. She yelled at Ritee pressing her jaws harder and started breathing like a pregnant cow.

"You didn't bother to think once Ritee before taking this bold and wild step. I have never thought my friend who used to advise us will fall in her own trap of idiosyncrasies. You didn't think about your family, your parents and not even me. Where did you sell your ideologies my dear?" And she narrated like a drama queen.

"Don't make me feel guiltier Sibangini? I did a mistake." Ritee mopped her runny nose while saying.

"Mistake, don't be so lenient."

"Okay, crime, now you are happy. And by the way what do you mean that I didn't think about you?" Ritee asked.

"Means, the Lady Casanova like me, mind it like me has never fallen into this shit. Arey, you don't know about typical male character. They will be ready to die for you till you are pure to them. But once they taste your purity, next time it stinks to them. Your love life finished. You got me." Sibangini narrated her idiotic philosophies for some more time which didn't solve the query at all, rather it made Ritee sobbed. The miserable look of Ritee enabled Sibangini to realize that it is easy to give philosophies to someone but it is too tough to empathize. She understood that her friend needs condolence now but on the contrary she is giving her high dose of nicotine. She tamed her frustration somehow and hugged Ritee to calm her down. And Ritee tried her best to hold the tears.

"By the way Ritee, how did you feel?" And Sibangini came to her ideal self being a jerk.

"What?"

"Did you feel the orgasm?"

"Means?"

"Arey stupid, did you feel like seeing stars . . . um . . . moon . . . . and . . . tasting honey, strawberry at the same time during love making," Sibangini told like a typical artist's speech of a drama by swinging her hands simultaneously.

"What are you saying Sibangini." And Ritee started weeping again.

"Ok, ok, calm down. It is a past now. But dear . . . one more thing, I don't know how you react. By any chance, if . . . you become pregnant . . . ?"

Ritee got absolutely frozen and looked like a corpse. The shocking implication of Sibangini made her cry relentlessly this time.

"No, no, please listen to me, don't . . . don't worry, we will do something." People get deeply hurt when someone touches their Achilles heel. But to be honest, Sibangini felt she pissed on Ritee's Achilles heel this time. Now she has to do something to wash it.

It is a bad habit of Ritee and Sibangini to skip the dinner and used to get it parcelled to their hostel room. They normally hate taking food in noisy canteen but today they hate to take food itself. Ritee, for her obvious reason but Sibangini was oddly waiting for Swati. Just to find out some solutions by the help of Swati's encyclopaedic knowledge on Biology.

"My dear Swati, how is the preparation for your exam going on?"

And Swati got fully flattered by Sibangini's buttering words. "Yeah, nice. But still some topics are left yaar."

"Shall we revise some chapters?"

"Sure. But, which one?"

"Let's start with Reproduction . . . ?"

"Okay." A studious Swati never dawdle to discuss studies and hence Sibangini tried to take the best advantage.

"When female ovary generates the egg?" Sibangini asked.

"What?" Swati got bemused.

"Yeah, what happened? Is this out of syllabus?"

"No no. It's there. Normally . . . it is between 08th-12th days after the completion of period."

"And when male generate theirs . . . ?"

Swati smiled and replied, "Stupid, it contains in their semen and lasts up to 3 days in female after . . . after . . . you know what . . . don't you? And it both gets fertilized if the copulations occur during this particular time."

"Oho . . . okay. Now it is cleared. I am very confused in Reproduction, seriously."

"But I know . . . you are very confident in performing action, aren't you?" Swati's reply made everybody laugh.

"Ok, good night then." Sibangini turned her head towards Ritee to take on some more gossips.

"Oh, hello madam, your revision is over. By the way, what made you to ask me all these specific questions, tell me? Tell me whether you have done something unhygienic, huh?"

"Haha, very funny." Sibangini smirked at Swati. After sometime when Chandrima and Swati slept, Ritee along with Sibangini came out of the hostel room and started analysing the logic given by Swati. They both started calculating the periodic cycle by using their fingers and tried to correlate its permutation & combination with Ritee's case. No knowledge is better than half knowledge sometimes. And they both fall prey to this myth as they could not normalise their heart beat even after putting various attempts to derive a solution. When it was late in the night they prepared themselves to be optimistic and went to sleep by keeping fingers crossed. Ritee could have erased one more vigilant night of her life if Swati would not have muttered those sentences.

"Sibangini, I did not tell you one more thing. There are some rarest breed on earth can fertilize in any days apart from their period time. So it is always better to consult a gynaecologist immediately after the action."

This comment made Ritee to wonder for the whole night, "Whether am I blessed with this nefarious power of being able to fertilize in any day of my life?"

Sibangini closely knows a gynaecologist whom she pronounces as Dr. Didi and her thought came to her mind in that terrible situation. They planned to consult Dr. Didi not only because of her experience, but knowing the secrets must be safe if they consult a much known Doctor.

"By the way, do you belong to the rarest breed category of Swati? I am sure you must be yaar. You are truly a character." Sibangini was not over yet.

"Oh stop it please. Don't make me tensed."

"Arey, just vacate your worries dear. Dr. Didi is renowned for these types of cases. She will not allow any adverse happen to you. I felt really better in the first day . . ."

"Means? When did you consult her?" Ritee looked shockingly sceptical and peered at Sibangini.

"Arey, no no. I just accompanied my sister in law," Sibangini replied. But her self-defence went futile when Dr. Didi welcomed her in a frustrating manner.

"What Sibangini, not again my child. I told you to take precautions last time."

"Didi, wait wait. She is the patient," Sibangini told by pointing at Ritee. But she knew she was caught red handed.

Dr. Didi raised doubts over Ritee's pregnancy after conducting few tests and recommended her few medicines to nullify the risk. But she still insisted Ritee to meet her, if her period gets missed next month. That day Ritee heaved a relief and laughed at Sibangini's response. Knowingly or unknowingly Sibangini's anecdote becomes the reason of her happiness. She knows that but today she accepted it and gave a kiss on her cheek.

"I love you Sibangini, thanks for bringing me here," Ritee said.

16

$\mathscr{I}$t had been three more weeks passed after Ritee consulted Dr. Didi but the trepidation of her mind still existed in some corner. And that day meant celebration to her when she got a timely period of the month. So far she has despised this incensed five days of every month in her life. But surely, today she realized the holy prominence of this crucial five days. And finally she got rid out of those insomniac nights. She had not been able to study neither had she concentrated on her personal life from last few weeks. She had lost her weight and was in a doomed state of mind. She felt losing her delicacy and censured it to the night of her virginity loss. And whenever Sibangini asks her about Srijesh, she repeats only one sentence.

"I will kill him if he ever comes my way."

"Really, what if you would have become the mother of his child?"

"For you it is very easy to say. Isn't it? I would have killed him for sure."

"Ok, that means you still want to meet him. Don't you?"

"Oh please. I think from today onwards we should stop discussing this topic." And they both had almost burnt it till a night when a small phone call dismantled them. It was a phone call for Sibangini in the night time. The intelligent caller knows about the lower unit rate during night, particularly for STD calls. That one seemed to be the longest duration call for Sibangini which certainly made Ritee uneasy. She could not circle her anxiety and propelled to ask about the caller details.

"You won't believe if I tell you the truth," Sibangini replied.

Ritee never bothers if somebody calls her friends for such long duration but this time she behaved differently.

"If I give you three chances, who do you pick?" Sibangini tried to play puzzle to sustain the curiosity of

Ritee's mind. Ritee pointed few incorrect names vaguely. She even named Prof. Ignesh who would be busy in his extended honeymoon. Srijesh's name strobed for a second in her mind but she kept it as the last option.

"Was it Sri . . . ?" Ritee apparently asked.

"Yes, yes, yes . . ."

Sibangini's answer gave her a thunderstruck. She felt highly unstable inside.

"I don't believe. Go and make others fool," Ritee said.

"I told already. You won't believe me."

Ritee knew Sibangini was not completed yet. If it was Srijesh's call, she will definitely elaborate. But what made him to call? How did he get the contact detail? Many baseless thinking stroked her mind till Sibangini narrated her discussion had with Srijesh.

"He was asking only about you Ritee. He has called only to know how you are. Just talk to him once. Please."

"Don't behave like his lawyer Sibangini."

"I am not. But I just want to make a clarification. It always takes two to make a quarrel. Mind it. If this disaster has happened, you are equally responsible my dear."

Even though Ritee believed it was Srijesh's call, she gave an ignorant look to Sibangini's request. Her look was so convincing that implied she doesn't damn care to speak to Srijesh anymore. But Srijesh was that person who made her seven days of journey truly remarkable. He showed her that there is a different life too exists in this world. A Life made of love and bliss. And those 'seven days' was truly a part of it. She started introspecting and asked herself, "Was she equally responsible?" As she released all the nightmares from her mind, she could clearly memorize that merciless night. What if she would have tied her foot not to meet Srijesh? It is she who came near to him fighting all odds. If Srijesh kissed her with passion she also invited him with a lusty pout. If Srijesh clasped her arms, she also scratched his back by her finger nails. If Srijesh ruffled her bra, she also tore his shirt button to retaliate. And if Srijesh laid her on the lap of the sand, she also spread her legs to reciprocate. She could have overcome the mayhem inside her and the cause of her sleepless nights.

But she did not. Then why she is behaving paranoid at this point of time as no such adverse consequence has happened after their intimacy. No, it is not correct at all. One thing has happened for sure. Now she can evoke the holy spirits of love making in each of her nerves. And she can't describe this ecstasy in one word, that much it worth for.

17

$\mathcal{I}$t would have been easier to spend time for Srijesh if he has not been getting a piece of seclusion. And during his lonesomeness he could not think anything other than Ritee. Life has never been so traumatic for him like last two months. Unreasonably, he tries to be occupied to get rid out of Ritee's thought but he is not able to succeed so far. He goes for his job, evening guitar class but there on he struggles to spend the night. So many weeks have gone by but he has not been able to hear Ritee's voice. Even though he called Sibangini few times but Ritee never appears over phone. He sometimes curses Ritee for her obsessive egotism but at the same time he appraises her boldness. He knows, he has wrecked the self-respect of this innocent girl and he would like to rectify his mistakes by extending her a lifelong commitment or even more. He does not care from where she belongs to; he does not care how she will be accepted by his family. All he cares about is his ceaseless love for Ritee.

He heard from Sibangini that they are over with their final term and are leaving for their respective natives very soon. From that day onwards the fear of losing Ritee kept on hounding him all the time.

In this sadness if he got some opportunities to steal some smile was because of his two bosoms Suju and Chotu. Chotu gave most of the time an ideal company as he was much aware of Srijesh's tormented situation. But Suju was becoming unbearable. While Srijesh being the guitar teacher became very close to Parker's family, Suju was keeping a reluctant distance from them. Of course it was personal one and not professional. He was still the chief supervisor in Parker's Hotel but he had switched his girlfriend then and had fallen for a vivacious African lady and they both were perfectly utilizing the hotel rooms in off season. But to experience a change, she came to Suju's house to quench her physical appetite on one fine night. But it was that night unfortunately, when Srijesh adjudged to tell his love story to Suju to seek some solutions. And finally he dropped the plan as Suju started introducing his girlfriend.

"Baby, meet Srijesh and Chotu, my younger brothers." Suju never introduced himself as an Uncle to Srijesh, just to hide his age to the girls. "And boys, she is . . . is . . . ummm . . . Angel . . . Angel," Suju baffled and one can clearly catch the reasons. Either he has forgot her name or not able to pronounce it.

"Who is Angel?" Now the lady perplexed in her own African tone.

"Darling, from today onwards I will call you Angel, you are my Sweet Angel." Suju kissed her head to flatter her, as he forgot the name.

"No. No. I will tell. I am Boitumelo Dubaku." Something she said in her mother tongue while everybody was eager to know her name. Finally they realized when Suju elucidated the meaning of what she said. It is the name of 'the joy of being the eleventh child of her parents.' Chotu and Srijesh looked astonishingly screamed. And chotu the super astute guy predicted that there might not be any facility of condom supply in her native.

"You said you are alone in the house. Are they going to join us?" Her question was filled with holy innocence but she told having a sad facial expression.

"No, no, no Baby. Don't be scared. We are three in the house, but I am the one for you. Look he is a child," pointing at Chotu he explained, "and the other fellow is in LOVE," pointing at Srijesh he tried to settle her down.

"LOVE." The lady surprisingly blushed as if she heard this word for the first time in life.

"Yes Baby, he is in deep love. Just leave him in his own fucking world. He is good for nothing." And Suju tried to mock being a highly disbeliever of love.

"Deep love. Wow. Baby, do you also do deep love to me?" The lady asked innocently again connecting her eyes straight towards Suju which left Srijesh and Chotu in an uncontrolled situation to laugh.

Suju looked fainted and replied, "I think you are drunk heavily, let's go inside."

"Okay, come on in." The ebony lady pulled Suju's collar and they entered the house in such a way that they are not going to step out of the king size bed until next day morning. That night Srijesh and Chotu could not sleep in the living room, neither they could sleep in veranda due to the high intensity of noise pollution made by Suju and his partner. But that sleepless night prompted Srijesh to write a letter to Ritee. A letter, which he wrote under the falling cascade of moon light, filled with copious amount of hopes where each word seeks a reply from her.

Dear Ritee,

It has been innumerable days passed but I have never found myself in a single moment without your memories. It is the memories of our first meeting, our friendship and our togetherness. I don't know how you feel about me, but my feelings for you are still the same and will be there always. I love you Ritee, I love you more than my life.

I know I have done a crime. I was cruel, but believe me Ritee I was never intent to. Don't leave me in a situation where I will repent throughout my life. Give me at least a chance to confess. Else I can't forgive myself.

I came to know from Sibangini that you all are leaving for your native soon. If you have ever accepted me as your friend, just talk to me once Ritee. And I promise, I will never come in your way.

Your unfortunate friend
Srijesh

He folded this letter in a lovely greeting card and drafted it to the address whose detail he has stolen from visitor's diary in Parker's Home stay.

18

What a number of phone calls could not do, the letter justified Srijesh's apology and his pursuit to speak to Ritee. That day was supposed to be the last day of the girls in their hostel. They insisted to do some adventure which will last for a long time after their college life. It is never easy for any of them to end three years journey of college life in one single day. During evening they sat to play cards followed by the 'Dare & Truth' game. And it was decided that the rule book will be exclusively given by the winner of the card game. All started praying Sibangini to lose; else she will molest everyone's sentiments with her absolute dirty questions in Dare & Truth. But the opposite happened and now Sibangini is the master to tame others in this ugly game. She will be asking eachone a weird question whose answer should be given only by two options, yes or no. And it is not over yet. If somebody says "no", then she has to perform the daring task given by Sibangini to convert it as "yes". And she attacked Swati first, for her part of question.

"To my dear Swati . . . now tell me if you have given a lip kiss to Chaterjee."

"Oh my God, when they progressed this much distance." Ritee thought of herself, being not able to realize, that others had gone too far when she was completely grasped by her bitter days.

And Swati replied, "Yes." And that too without any hesitation which implied they both were seeing each other from a long time leaving Ritee's thought way behind.

The second victim was Chandrima who got fired with an outrageous question which Ritee has never dreamt about. Atleast for Chandrima's case.

"To my dear Chandrima . . . now tell me, have you ever masturbated inside our room?"

"No, no, no." Chandrima shrieked but finally bowed down to Sibangini's staring look.

101

"Ok, yes . . . but it is only once huh. Else I prefer to do in wash room always." Perhaps Chandrima realized it is better to be honest than to perform the daring task in front of everybody.

And finally it was Ritee's turn which Sibangini was insatiably waiting for. Ritee looked frightened and started praying to avoid the rough question of Sibangini. She was determined; if Sibangini asks any weird question related to Srijesh, she will reveal Sibangini's secrets. But she denied the idea as they both belong to the same trap. And she got victimised when Sibangini asked, "Do you love the Goan guy, Srijesh?"

"No."

"Are you sure?"

"Damn sure?"

"Ok, don't blame me then, you have to speak to him once over phone."

"Huh! Bullshit, why do I?"

"Rule is rule Baby. You have to obey me at any cost tonight."

Chandrima and Swati were clueless about this argument being unknown to the real fact. But Swati spoke like an intelligent girl, "If you don't love him, then what bothers you to speak to him? I feel this is the easiest task Sibangini has given you." Poor girl doesn't know the difficulty level for Ritee to speak to that person . . . that person who has stolen everything from her.

"Yeah, so let's clap for Ritee." Sibangini cheered and was anxious to see the most romantic play when Ritee will be speaking to Srijesh. But nobody knows the secret; it is Sibangini who has already updated Srijesh to call that night to their hostel number.

Ritee had not been able to renovate her traumatized mind after the incident and how come she will suddenly speak to Srijesh who she had considered as the culprit behind it. Her heartbeat again stroke faster in this spooky situation and breath seemed in a verge to finish. She tried to subdue all the acrimony inside her heart and forcibly spoke to Srijesh against her will. She was nervous, however Srijesh felt like cresting the Great Himalayas when he heard Ritee's voice after a long . . . long time. He had concealed his lost hope to speak to Ritee in some corners of his heart and as he got the opportunity, he leaked it entirely during this phone call. He talked for a long time as he got enough reasons to speak, unlike Ritee who kept on searching for words to reply. She barely recollected Srijesh words in this inapt conversation except one request, for which she was not having any answer.

"Ritee, shall I be able to speak to you if you go to your native?" Srijesh didn't mind at all being shameless and asked, whose answer he received in a form of hazy silence from Ritee. They both don't know if they can be connected with each other in any mode of communication in future. However, they both felt a reason of complacency. Srijesh was fulfilled from inside as Ritee's words seemed unapologetic. And Ritee might not have forgiven Srijesh but she accepted him as a part of her small world.

19

$\mathcal{N}$ext day all the girls left for their respective natives. Swati and Sibangini caught their first train towards Darjeeling. Chandrima left for her hometown which is in a suburban area of Kolkata. Most of the girls don't know from where Ritee actually belongs to. She happened to be one of the most reticent and conservative girls, but nobody knows the reason behind it. She has never detailed about her family to any of her friends, neither has she invited any of them to her home. She herself kept aloof from others, being a girl child from highly orthodox family. She loved Kolkata where she feels free from all bondage of her family's hollow traditions.

She arrived at Midnapore Station and walked under the scorching sun of summer to catch the last bus to her native. She purchased her ticket to the last stoppage and occupied the reserved seat for ladies. She likes to keep her head down for the entire journey. One after another people stepped out but she didn't dare to look outside. Keeping her face partially closed by her chunri, she finished her lunch when the bus stopped for a while. She never prefers to offer her side by seat to strangers, but likes to occupy the window seat even at the cost of inhaling polluted dust. She was bound to get down at the last stop and walked towards the river bank. Keeping her palms closed under her belly she waited for the old boatman till he finishes his job and accompanies her to home. Each step she moved further she felt clung by some unholy forces of the village graveyard. She tried to avoid the sarcastic comments and vigorous eye contact of the insane youth near to the Beetle shop. And in the late evening when the stars started twinkling, she reached her house situated in the remote coastal village on the West Bengal and Orissa border.

Ritee has never received a welcome from her family members. Sometimes her father forges a smile on her home coming and asks few things about her studies, college etc. merely as formality. He is a small time businessman and an owner of some nominal farm land. Most of the people including Ritee know that his liabilities are much more than his assets. But Ritee feels indebted to her father as he allowed her to complete her graduation at least. She loves him most in the entire family and it is purely by force being a motherless child. She lost her mother at the age of ten and from there on she didn't find anybody of her own in the house. Sometime she curses her father who brought a stepmother for her. She starves for the motherly affection but was not blessed to receive the same ever, as that woman was never free from nourishing her own boy child, Ritee's so called brother who was at a tender age of seven. Moreover their family consists of an old couple who are her grandparents and they have never loved Ritee. Simple reason was that she is a girl and a burden for their family. If they ever see Ritee bypass them, they ask about their maiden wish, her marriage.

In this entire suffocating environment inside the two rooms and a veranda house, she feels reposed near to her mother's photograph hung in the corner most places. Apart from burning time in kitchen and studies, she spends long hours watching it.

Ritee's life would have been shrugged with same pace till she got a do or die situation of her life. Either she had to get married or find a source of income to support her father. But it was not at the cost of returning to Kolkata once again. She was destined to go for the second option, as she got a job as an ad-hoc teacher in a primary school situated on the other side of the river. She tried to circle her life running from her home to school and vice versa.

Now she loves to sleep alone in the gloomy night which allows her to foster some idyllic memories of her past. Few memories make her smile, but she feels the night worthier when some of them tantalise her. Now she loves to brush her fingers throughout her body and feels being undulated with every blow of cold wind. She loves to clasp her bosom and feels the warmth of Srijesh. Now she loves to sleep naked during thunderous monsoon nights and feels titillated by hearing the soothing voice of rain drops. She feels sensuous when the black clouds clash each other and produce some shuddering sounds of intimacy. She stands near to the open window and invites the dancing bubble to fall on her chest and cement the smouldering desire emerges during rainy nights. She feels being completely imbibed by her erotic thoughts and craves for Srijesh to submit herself every time. The act what she has confessed as a despicable crime, now she desires to commit it again and again with Srijesh. Is this the same stage for Ritee arrives which every beautiful girl gets threatened of, where their conscience gets hopelessly defeated by their dark sexual fantasies? And finally that night stood where she roused from her light sleep and bothered the pen and paper.

Dear Srijesh,

I could not reply to your last letter. But the truth is I don't know what to write. From the beginning you are honest to me in expressing all your feelings. I wish I could have shown the same nuances of honesty with you. I don't know by the time you receive my letter, you would have changed your feelings for me. If that is so, I am the most unfortunate girl. And you have every right to do that. But if not, then you will have all the opportunities from me for a new beginning.

Now I am in home with my entire family. Yet I feel lonely sometimes. And the very reason is you. You showed me a life which I had only dreamt about. Every beat of those seven days were so enticing that I just have to close my eyes and those seem dancing in front of me. Those seven days are truly world to me. I have never thanked you for that from the bottom of my heart. I don't know what will be my future. What God has decided about my fate? But if I get one more opportunity then I will go to your place.

You are a nice guy Srijesh. Be the way you are. You were right in your letter. Every mistake can be wiped out by admitting it candidly. And you can do it by replying my letter.

Yours
Ritee

And this time she not only wrote her name but mentioned her contact number and address where she was working.

20

$\mathcal{I}$t was a new sunrise in Srijesh's life when he received Ritee's letter. He had almost granted his life of complacency without Ritee, but the letter incremented the expectancy from his own love for Ritee. Now he is damn confident that there is a life which is clogged with her and believes Ritee will be his undoubtedly. For him, she is the girl with whom he can spend rest of his life or even more . . . if God blesses him. That day he took a day off from work and became the first attendant in church prayer. He wished every known and unknown person with a perky smile. He lighted a candle and prayed for Ritee. It was none of the any auspicious days, but for him that day was having a strong meaning in his life. That day his love blossomed like an autumn flower by obeying the orders of the season change. It was certainly the season of love for him. He waited for the afternoon time when Ritee had asked him to call. He called exactly when the office hours expired and heard Ritee's voice after a long time. It sounded exactly the same like when they both were less known to each other, when they were beginning their relationship and when there was no hesitation in speaking to each other.

Now almost every day they speak, and if by any chance they can't, they pen their feelings in the form of letters. In few occasions when they can't, they spend their times in reading each other's letters. And in between this if they pull away some time, they love to recollect their words.

You know Srijesh, I hid your letter and read it nearby sea coast. I can sense our days of togetherness sitting on the sea sand.

Even I feel you Ritee, when I run down the beaches, the water, the sand and looking at the moon who has witnessed our togetherness.

How do you feel Srijesh, do you see me there.

I kiss the lap of the sand Ritee, where we made love.

Oh Srijesh, don't make me blush.

Really, are you? How do you look Ritee?
Just close your eyes, Can you feel me Srijesh?
I feel you are my life Ritee.
You are my strength to fight the whole world Srijesh.
I want to embrace you Ritee.
I want to lean on your chest Srijesh.
I want to hold you Ritee.
I do want to feel protective by hiding under your arms Srijesh.
I want to kiss your eyes.
I want to see yours to feel myself charming in your eyes.
I love you Ritee. Your's Srijesh.
I love you too Srijesh. Your's and only your's Ritee.

On her first month of salary date, Ritee went to the town market and bought something for her family members. She eagerly bought one shirt for Srijesh in her hard earned money and took the privilege in sending it to him. And when she realized of some money still left, she called Srijesh from a nearby telephone booth.

Every time one new excuse from Ritee suppressed Srijesh's decision of meeting and every time she succeeded to calm him down. She even sent him one photograph which acted like a temporary treatment to his afflicted state of mind. From the day Srijesh received the photograph, he used to spend time doing nothing but looking at it. When he finds himself alone, he kisses it numerous times. Though only one photograph, but it helps him to overcome his sluggish days. Srijesh knew . . . somebody has to take the initiative and being the stronger sex of their relationship, he decided to ask for a meeting at any cost. It is not that he hasn't tried to ask before, but every time Ritee takes it for granted. And finally Srijesh cited his desperation to meet Ritee against her objection. Ritee denied as she is still unsettled to lift the next step of her love life. But she knows, they both have come a long way in their relationship and now she will be called treachery, if she steps back. In between Ritee got two weeks off during Dussehra holidays. Now there is no reason for her to go to the town except to call Srijesh. It was the longest duration gap they have spoken to each other. She has not answered profoundly to Srijesh in their last call. Neither could she explain about her insoluble dilemma being in native. She could only insist Srijesh to wait for the right time, even though she knows that they both are suffering every second of their separation.

21

$\mathcal{I}$n Kolva, that was a memorable day in Suju's mansion when he brought two brand new scotch bottles in the evening. It was evident from his eyes that either he has got a part time job with high return on investment or he has found a fresh night partner. Chotu was about to lick when he saw the expensive scotch bottles and started sourcing the requirements to garnish for a colourful evening. Srijesh decided to get sedated for giving a suspension to Ritee's thought which has covered him all the time. Also Srijesh could read Suju's expression. He saw the rage in his eyes for some dubious reasons which were going to blast against him.

Chotu dropped the ice cubes in scotch glasses along with soda and handed over the respective glasses to Srijesh and Suju. Though after a long time they were sitting together for drinks, being absorbed in their own lives, they didn't forget to say, "Cheers."

"So . . . Chotu Ustad. How is your love life going on man?" Suju initiated his most hatred topic of love as a lethal weapon. Though it was asked to Chotu but the gunpoint was targeted towards Srijesh.

"Arey, leave it Guru. I don't think that girl is worth for a shot."

"Why?"

"She is still incapable at the receiving end." Chotu started speaking philosophical. Perhaps the scotch was too strong for him to handle.

"So what are you going to do?" Suju asked.

"I will change her."

Their conversation seems premeditated as Chotu was acting like a trumpet to elaborate Suju's ideas.

"Fanstastic. That is called a smart move. A manly move. You know, there are some people in the world never learn by seeing other's mistakes. They patiently wait for their turn to fall in the dig. And a proud example is sitting amongst

110

us." Suju's eccentricity seems deliberately killing Srijesh's emotion.

"Why are you not talking straight to me Uncle?" Srijesh joined in the rapid fire round.

"Are you in a position to talk? You are going to become a loser in love, do you realize it? Chotu, just educate your friend man." Suju said.

Chotu thought it will be a wise decision to keep quiet as he speculated a Mahabharat to happen between these blood relations. Without interfering, he started making exclusive pegs for himself.

"Why Chotu will tell? You come straight to the point Uncle."

"Fine then. Now tell me, what satisfaction you are getting from that Bengali girl. What are you expecting from her? Do you realize your future?"

"Yes I do. I am planning to meet her soon," Srijesh answered.

"And what will happen in that? Boy, just for few seconds of satisfaction you are going a long way to West Bengal and that too without expecting any fruits. I will give you a better deal man. I can arrange more entertainment for you here. It will save your cost and effort simultaneously." Suju threw his petulant opinions.

"Shit. I feel dejected at your filthy remarks Uncle. I love her. I repeat, I love her," Srijesh started justifying.

"Oh my great Romeo. You young generation don't know anything about love. You see a girl, speak few filmi languages and roam for sometimes holding each other's hand and conclude it as love. Fuck off man. Love means there should not be any conditions; there should not be any boundary. Whenever you call your partner, she should care and ready to be in bed with you. This girl is wasting your time, money and energy. These small town girls will never allow you before marriage. They suck you till they get exasperated. If still something is pending after their exhaustion, they ask you to marry. If not, they suck another guy." He heaved a relief and again resumed, "I also loved Julie, a beautiful Goan girl. I worshipped her like a goddess and never ever tried to

111

touch her for my physical benefit. And what happened. She left me when her marriage got fixed with a rich Doctor. And even today, I realize I should have fucked her at least once." Suju said by carrying a plethora of bereft in his voice. The story was not new to Srijesh but this time he could smell its honesty. And the honesty spilled as a flow of tear in Suju's eyes.

To defend himself Srijesh was about to disclose his relation with Ritee and how far they have gone. He has even achieved from Ritee, what is so called the meaning of love in Suju's language. But how can he muscle the self-respect of the girl who he loves more than his life.

"You are a loser Uncle."

The small sentence left Suju sulked for a while. Chotu realized the time has come to offer a strong drink to his Guru.

"Just because a girl left you, you are having no rights to spoil other's image." Srijesh further added and the war of words continued till the final sentence hit, which froze Suju completely.

"I want to marry her."

"You want to marry her. Have you blown out of your fucking mind? Do you know which caste, which religion she belongs to?"

And finally Srijesh realized, he has to be an animal to counter attack the other animal Suju and he asked, "Do you think about religion while getting intimate with a woman? Certainly not I believe."

The last peg and the last sentence of Srijesh went hand in hand and finally Chotu was bound to offer the whole bottle to Suju, seeing him losing the battle.

Suju gawked blank as the liquor smote his emotional quotient and he asked, "So what have you planned? Is she inviting you to meet her parents?"

"No, not yet. She is asking me to wait for the right time," Srijesh replied which brought a scary smile on Suju's face.

"Right time. Fuck off. My dear, I will give you a suggestion. If you wait for the final call from your girlfriend, you will end up nowhere. It is always better to follow your heart than the stupid girls. Mind it."

"If you were in my place, what you would have done?"

"At least I would not be masturbating like you. I would have abducted her from her family." Suju sounded like a rapist but his courageous ideologies instigated Srijesh to try for the impossible. He waited for the next day morning and woke up to a new surprise. He saw a sheet of paper and some money left in a wallet. Suju follows his usual style whenever he wants to offer some money or gift to Srijesh. Srijesh has to bury his false notion of disbelieving Suju. Till last night he was thinking that Suju will never allow him to go. Else it will be following the path of love, which he never votes. But this letter contradicted his view point where it was written:

BOSS, YOU OWED ME COMPLETELY. TAKE THIS MONEY AND BUY TRAIN TICKET. GO AND BRING YOUR LOVE. MY BEDROOM IS YOURS TILL YOU FINISH YOUR HONEYMOON. FORGET BED, MY WHOLE HOUSE IS YOURS. NOW I KNOW LOVE IS THE MOST IMPOTENT PART OF LIFE. ENJOY.

Srijesh smiled as he knew, Suju meant to write 'love is the most important part of life'. It is not that one fine night some miracle happened and shelved Suju's petulance, but the fact is, he loves to see Srijesh happy all the time, till he is alive.

22

$\mathcal{S}$rijesh declared even though Ritee opposes him; he would still continue his journey to West Bengal. He can't predict anything for a winning conclusion till he meets Ritee. This time he is not just going to meet her but he knows this journey will decide his fate. What Ritee meant over phone and her letter, whether she poses the equal courage to accept him. He wants to see and believe. And if all goes in his favour, he will abduct her. That is what he learnt from Suju and wanted to finalize it. From yesterday he tried his best to organise some Jasmine flowers and made a gift wrap. Ritee likes Christmas cake, so he packed some scrumptious handmade Goan sweets for her. And a beautiful Goan dress he bought, pink colour which suits Ritee best. He was behaving like an obsessive lover and if somebody asks him what is his aim of life, that day he would have answered, "It is to marry Ritee." And he was ready to fight against any living or non-living super power if it obstructs his way.

Chotu being a loyal friend accompanied Srijesh. Suju gave him a handful amount of money to ensure them a smoother and successful journey. If Suju was permitted, he would have put vermillion tilak on Srijesh's forehead to wish him win the love battle. And Chotu for one point of time correlated themselves as the characters of epic Ramayana when lord Rama and Laxman go to save Maa Sita and triumph the war of love, truth and respect.

For the first time in life Srijesh wanted to touch Suju's feet to take his blessings but dropped the plan to avoid looking over dramatic. But Suju created a drama when he cried at Srijesh, while train was about to leave, "Srijesh, bring her home at any cost, else don't come back to Goa, Go to Kerala from there on." His voice went unheard as the siren bell rang. Srijesh left with Chotu to cram the mission of his life.

Srijesh felt half-hearted for not been able to go to the church as he hastened for the station in early morning. But when one by one station passed, he regained his enthusiasm. Every ten minute makes him to look at the watch impatiently though he knows he has not even crossed half of the journey time. Looking at Ritee's photograph he tries to cerebrate for some romantic techniques to surprise her. He could not devoid of thinking how she might react? Whether she will hug him in public? Whether she will grant for a kiss when they will be lonely? Whether Ritee will invite him to her family or he has to opt for the daunting steps like a film hero. He seems completely envisaged by his fantasies while trying to sleep inside the train. It makes him to wake up every alternate hour. He voluntarily sacrifices his reserved seat to some old people. He tries to be generous and donates ten rupee notes to beggars roaming inside the train. Whichever girls he sees inside the train, he treats them like his sisters and he never tries to look at them below their neck. But whenever he sees any ticket collector, he politely asks the rubbish question, "Train is in right time sir?" And before sleeping he wanted to reconfirm, "When shall we reach Midnapore Station sir?"

"No idea. Train will be late due to some problem."

It was a deceptive answer for him and he wanted to interrogate further, "What problem sir?"

And the Ticket Collector rushed from there without answering.

With closed eyes in subconscious mind, Srijesh was trying to sleep some more time. Outer world was looking dark referring the stage would be of early morning. If not, it will be 6 o' clock maximum. Wiping his eyes, Srijesh looked at his wrist watch and got surprised. He tapped it few times but realized it is in working condition showing time of 10.30. AM or PM no idea. He rotated his eyeballs around the train compartment and saw only a few numbers of passengers sitting inside the train. They were quiet and shivering. Train was kept on halt for a long time.

"Chotu, wake up, something wrong."

"Hmmm." Chotu can hardly open his eyes but came to his normal condition by looking at the unusual scenario. They both cornered towards the boggy gate and the moment they opened it, saw something which could easily take their breath away. The slow and buzzing sound of wind, audible inside the train, has transformed into a humungous and scary tone. And the black clouds looked perilous than ever.

Oh . . . my . . . God. It was darker than the character of a slut.

Passengers gathered on the rail track looked chaotic. Wind seemed blowing at its maximum speed and crowd felt getting continuously displaced from their places. It showed nobody got strength to look at the sky which seems tearing apart and can fall anytime. Dark clouds were grudging at monstrous voice leaving all the people in a bizarre state of life. Following everybody Srijesh and Chotu too started cursing themselves as a part of this haunted situation.

From a railway staff Chotu came to know that train will stop here for infinite time. Certain causes were unclear and the train was resting in some parts of Orissa. For them every second was valuable as they have to travel hundred more miles to reach their destination. Hardly bothered about the current scenario Srijesh fondled his pocket to bring out a sheet of paper where Ritee's address was written.

"It is far from here. You can go up to Balasore and from there on you need to rely on road transport."

His voice gets suppressed when an old man told in an arguing voice, "Jai paribani, batya, bhayankar batya."

Srijesh ignored the old man's words and kept on asking about the route direction. The rail staff got stunned and translated what the old fellow told, "You can't go further, a super cyclone has hit badly."

And Chotu thought, "Which enemy's name is Super Cyclone."

With a complete absent mind Srijesh and Chotu sat beside the rail track. They heard people talking to their respective local languages and felt being forbidden from the crowd. They blindly followed some crowd and walked aimlessly for an hour or two. They reached Balasore town at the mid of afternoon with a complete void of sunray. The roads look deserted and town looks highly reclusive. And whoever was seen in that locality carry the unanimous topic of 'super cyclone' in their mouth. Everybody has got an open ended question but no solution attached to it. Srijesh asked many people about the direction to go to Ritee's place, but he got only a blatant smile in reply. Road transportation was totally messed. It seemed afternoon at least in the watch and they both realized they have not had food from yesterday. They tasted the ugliest food of their life in a small hotel. One good thing they heard that people can be participants in Red Cross bus which was providing relief to the cyclone affected areas. Without any second thought, Srijesh and Chotu stepped in and got two tags of Volunteers. And from there on Srijesh's journey started to search his love, his life Ritee. He did not take out his eyes off whereas other social workers were terrified to face the outer world. The bus did not stop till it reached the maximum distance it could cover.

Srijesh felt like a dumb observer among the volunteers. He could hardly make out, what others were speaking, being unknown to the vernacular language. They progressed farther barring any specific aim. The mission for others might be a rescue operation but for him it was to meet Ritee. More they progressed towards the coastal belt, more their eyes attracted the visual of widespread destructions. They did not stop even in the night. Hammered by the tremendous blow of wind it was almost impossible to walk alone. They progressed holding the support of one another's hand. Holding the fire stick in one hand they walked inside the route of a dense forest. When majority of people lacked their stamina, they managed to find a place to sleep in the night. And after few walks in the early morning, they saw what was beyond any explanation, beyond any imagination of a conjurer. It was illegal, a ruthless punishment to mankind.

Hundreds of houses were destroyed; thousands of people lives perished and monster from the sky seemed laughing at this pathetic situation of earth. Somewhere a father has lost his child and somewhere the child has become motherless. Somewhere a master has lost his entire property. There was no chasm between a rich and poor, where everyone had lost everything. There was no difference between human and animal, where their corpses lay in an inch distance. And whosoever blessed with their lives, they don't want to live it either.

Srijesh has read in books, whoever commits any sin will go to hell after dying. What these people have done and what difference this place is from hell. It is not possible that thousands of people have committed same crime and become cruel at one particular time. "Oh God, Are you biased to show clemency to your own handmade creatures," he grumbled.

"Babu . . . Babu . . ."

A middle aged woman cried at Srijesh by extending her palms. She looked similar to the age of his mother and was seeking for some food or water. Srijesh could not do anything for a while and later brought a packet of food. The old woman snatched the food packet and started eating as if she was engulfed by an animal instinct. She was barely able to chew and coughed several times during swallowing it. For a moment Srijesh's heart turned dysfunctional when the old woman touched his feet after being saved by him. Some volunteers started distributing packed water to the victims and some including Chotu and Srijesh started giving food parcels. Srijesh closed his eyes when he noticed a lady whose blouse was torn making his bosom completely visible. Without caring for self-respect she removed her sari to catch the food thrown at her while her two children had lost their lives and lain naked beside her. Srijesh was about to vomit when he saw an old man extending his one hand to take the food parcel whereas his other hand was trying to cover his genital.

Srijesh turned blind in his thoughts and vision. All these dreaded situations left him mooning for the reason he has come here. He felt being caged and powerless. He completely lost his cognitive state of mind. Where will hc go and search Ritee? Nobody is left with seconds to guide him. He was scared to visualize any adverse things for Ritee. Whether she is also a victim of this merciless cyclone? Whether she is also lying somewhere and craving for some food and water? The horrifying thoughts made him to open his wallet to see Ritee's photograph for a while. A drop of tear fell down from his eye. Looking at the hundred rupee note in the wallet, for the first time in life he realized it as a worthless substance. It can't even content the basic needs of human in this crucial time. And people are dying outside for its empowerment. Holy shit.

He prayed God to shower some miracles. "God, you take whatever you want from me. But save Ritee," he prayed to gain some potency. No matter he dies or lives, he marched further. For him that person was an angel who guided him through the direction towards Ritee's village. He did not bother to empty half of the weight of his wallet to that person. Without consuming any more tears he marched further. He was determined to save Ritee from devil's eye, even at the cost of losing his own life. He kept on giving blind assurance that Ritee will be alive and he will find her soon.

They stopped after walking few more miles when the companion told, "This is where the village was . . ."

Srijesh shivered when he saw his narrow vision of expectation got brutally fragmented. The place was devastated in such a way that any sensible person can ever say, "There was a village existed here." His legs flinched and resulted a feeling like his bones got completely dissolved. He fell down like a child and was devoid with any strength to crawl on the soil. He felt himself like the weakest person alive in the world. Chotu befriended by holding his shoulders and tried to give some fruitless condolence.

"Let's go Bhaiya. It will be night after sometime." By telling so Chotu pulled Srijesh and they left disrupted from that place. He felt like ending his quest for Ritee and lost her from his life. They came back to the NGO camp. Srijesh has completely paralyzed his voice and has not been able to speak to Chotu. Chotu offered him some food, knowing he has not taken anything from morning. Every bite he takes he realizes its bitterness can save somebody from starvation. He looked around and saw a small child smiling at him by looking at the jasmine flower. He handed over the flowers and the sweets what he has brought for Ritee and smiled for the first time in past few days.

Crushing all hopes of desperation, Srijesh left the place next day morning. He seeks to wipe all his memories of last four days. Every moment of the journey which he has worshiped, he likes to erase it from his lifelong memory. And he remembers only those few sentences of the last conversation had with Ritee.

"Ritee, what if I suddenly appear in front of you?"

"Hmmm . . . I will hug you first."

"And . . ."

"Then I will kiss you."

"And then . . ."

"That's it. Don't be over demanding ok."

"Ok, ok. I should not expect more."

"Hey . . . don't be. You have all the rights to expect from me. Because . . ."

"Because . . ."

"I love you."

23

*W*hile going back a small phone call of Chotu changed their direction from Goa to Mahe. They tried calling Suju but the phone went unanswered. When they called the hotel number, they came to know; urgently Suju had to rush to Mahe, as one of his relatives is unwell. And Suju has insisted them to come home directly once they receive the information.

The cyclone in Bay of Bengal has affected entire India it seems as it was raining in Mahe too. Partially drenched in light shower Srijesh reached his native. After a long time he was going to his native and that too without informing anyone. Else his father would have come to the station to receive him. His home, situated in corner most part of Mahe, enriches with loneliness and tranquillity. He thanked God for bringing him to Mahe so that he can spend some time and able to forget the anguish of his heart. He might get back those heydays by spending some valuable time with family. He can be a mischief playing with his little sister, he can have a good cook food prepared by his mother and play cards with his father along with some political discussions. Above all Suju is there. His presence itself is enough, being a magician of laughter. And Suju, as expected, appeared in front of Srijesh but didn't greet him with his unusual style. May be he was still upset with Srijesh as his approval of allowing him to go to West Bengal was not wholeheartedly. Walking inside the veranda of his house, he saw his mother in moist eyes. But he was surprised to see his little sister who didn't give a crooked smile on his arrival.

He found his mother, sister, uncle and the whole family and finally searched for his father. His father has always been the main support in restructuring his dampens morale. He searched here and there vehemently but could not find him. He could not see the face which welcomes him first; he could not see the hand that has always supported him. He could

121

not see his father now, neither can he in future. He looked at Suju who broke out loudly and fell on his shoulder. He said, "Sorry son. We waited for you. But it was too late. We buried him already."

Suju's words seem self-cursing. For half of his life he has disliked his brother and fate turns him being the sole companion performing the last rites. He believed it was supposed to be Srijesh's and he stole it from him. He was scared of facing Srijesh's eyes which must be demanding all its rights. However, Srijesh's eyes looked completely dry. Perhaps he was left with no more tears in it. He looked like a stone who can challenge all evils' power to destroy him. Just few days back Srijesh thought he is the luckiest person in the world. He has got his caring family and a lover Ritee and his life is complete. But how soon life has shown him the back and he feels so deprived like a beggar who can never see happiness in future. He could remember the words he has prayed to God, "You take whatever you want from me, but save Ritee." And God took his father. But is it at the cost of saving Ritee? He doesn't know. All he knows now is that two persons are totally dependent on him, his mother and his little sister. He knows neither can he run out of his responsibilities nor can he return Goa where he will asphyxiate in Ritee's memories. He feels like living on the edge of a sword in this situation till he receives a job reference in Middle East by one of his childhood friends. He realizes now that time has come to broad his shoulders and to balance his liabilities. Hundreds of useless attempts of Suju to call him back to Goa went unheeded, when he decided to go to the Middle East to start a new phase of his life.

Perhaps Srijesh is not aware but everyone knows he has a strong heart. He did not break though shattered from inside. He believes God the same way he has believed from the beginning. Last day in Mahe, he went to the church and prayed for his father's soul and for his love Ritee.

"Dear God. Bless my father's soul and take care of Ritee, wherever she is, just take care of her."

And he left to write his future in a new world.

24

$\mathcal{D}$ays turned into months and months turned into years. For four long years Srijesh had chosen a life of sacrifice, ignominy and dejection for him. He had abandoned all kinds of human pleasure required for a living life. Rather it was a life of a saint, where every second he constantly battled against an ascetic fear of falling down. Influenced by a friend, along with work he pursued his higher studies as well. Being away from his family he reckoned the value of money and his future responsibilities. He knew, he has a long way to go and prior to that he wants to stand tall. Once a year during Christmas, he goes to Mahe and tries to be as social as possible. But he never dares to visit Goa. He has burnt entire chapters of Goa from his unstructured life but could not tear the page where Ritee's name is written. When he realized he has got sufficient back up in terms of money, he decided to go back to his home. Now he can think about his sister's marriage, one of his major responsibilities being the eldest son of the family. From the past few months Suju is critically ill and he is staying in his departed place Mahe. But he has patiently waited for Srijesh to come and take him back to Goa once again. Friends say he is replete with adultery and very soon inviting his demise. Now Suju also knows his fate that he will be travelling to hell very soon. And before going, he wants to consume all heavenly pleasure in his much-loved place Goa. He is dying each of the moment because of the guilt inside and the discrimination he has faced. He never forced Srijesh to come back to Goa but he knows, Srijesh is the dearest one who will definitely fulfil his wish and that happened to be true. Srijesh took Suju along with him to Goa for spending few days of hopelessness.

Goa has never looked so sultry before as if nature has soaked all the sweetness of this place. Srijesh prediction of passing few unobjectionable days became tougher as he can still feel the joy and pain this place has offered him. He was wrong that time could heal the wounds of the past. Trying to sabotage the pain inside, he zeroed in on taking care of Suju. And in reply, Suju also tried to offer him the best escort he could give. He knows, Srijesh likes mutton gravy and he travelled to Margaon city market to buy fresh mutton. He patiently stood in a long queue in liquor shop to buy Srijesh's favourite drinks. Even after hundreds of opposition, Suju cooked for him. And even today he didn't forget to offer him the first bite. And when Srijesh's eyes look brimming with a large drop of tear, he politely said, "Don't worry man, this disease will not spread by touching."

Srijesh realized that day that human beings pose the astounding power of smiling even when deeply hurt. And after few seconds of silence Suju resumed, "Srijesh, let's forget everything. Till the time you are here, let's be like the way we were, what you say."

"Ok, Uncle." Srijesh tried to be well mannered.

They had a lovely but a tasteless dinner. Suju offered a glass of wine to Srijesh and they occupied two chairs facing the sea shore.

"Arey, you didn't ask about Chotu?"

"Yeah, I was supposed to. Where is he and how is his life by the way?" Srijesh showed an inquisitive feeling to know about Chotu.

"Haah, a film story man."

"Why, what happened to him. Is he alright?"

"Surprise . . . our Chotu master finally ran with that Mangalorean's daughter."

"Really. I don't believe you."

"Arey, trust me, it has been more than a year. And I am sure they will not come back till that girl becomes pregnant."

"Oh. Come on Uncle. That girl was in 7th standard when I was here. She must be 15 or 16 now."

And then Suju smiled upto his highest strength and Srijesh presumed for one more shocking twist in the tale.

"Arey, forget that girl. He grabbed that girl's elder sister."

"What?" And Srijesh sandwiched his tongue and pressed his hand on his forehead.

"Haha, that's what I am telling no. He is our Chotu master."

"What Mangalorean did then? He didn't file any police complaint or something?"

"What fucking complaint will he give? He would have, if his daughter is a minor. But here case is opposite. Our chotu master is a minor it seems and if he files complaint, police will arrest his daughter instead of arresting Chotu."

Srijesh laughed wholeheartedly after a long time and said, "Uff, what that girl saw in our chotu master Uncle."

"Wrong question; ask me what she didn't see. She saw everything of Chotu's and finally ran with him post her satisfaction."

"Crazy people Uncle, crazy world. Seriously." Srijesh's laughter doubled and Suju followed him. For a fraction of time, Suju felt at least Chotu's love story gratified Srijesh. And he is inundated with gladness because today also he loves to see Srijesh smiling.

Days passed by and now the doctors have given up already. They didn't signal for any hope left for Suju's ailment. His smile is faded and his colour is paled. His never-ending jokes are about to finish and whichever is left can hardly give any more smile. Now Suju is confirmed that he is left with some countable days. He is not having any more reasons or rights to stop Srijesh. He knows he is wasting Srijesh's valuable times, which he can invest somewhere else where hopes exist, unlike here. Indirectly he has hinted Srijesh to leave him and go back, but Srijesh didn't move at all leaving Suju alone in Goa. He has lost already one job offer for the sake of Suju and Suju can't forgive himself if he loses one more. It is to be a lecturer in a Business school in Bangalore. And one night Suju wanted to be scrupulous against his wish.

"Did you talk to your friend in Bangalore?"

"Huh . . . why?"

"Next month 1st is yours joining date no?"

"Again . . . we can speak about it later Uncle. Just sleep now." Srijesh showed his lack of interest in this conversation.

"Arey, don't worry about me man. I will not die till I see your children. God never invites scoundrel like me so soon."

"Can we mute this topic please? Just shut up and sleep." Srijesh became strict and serious.

"Ok, ok." Suju gave a glass of water to Srijesh. Even today he loves to take care of him the way he used to do earlier. And he swapped the topic of discussion instantly.

"Do you know, you have got two marriage proposals?"

"Really, and who are those two luckless girls?" Srijesh smiled and asked casually.

"You don't know. I hope your mother would have told you. Anyways, one girl is from Kochi, a single daughter from a family of bureaucrats. And the second one is a software engineer in Bangalore. Why don't you meet them? As you are going to Bangalore, just meet the second girl at least," Suju advised.

"Ok, I will meet them. Now will you please sleep? Doctor has given strict instructions for you."

Srijesh was least bothered about the marriage proposals and he has hardly ever imagined a girl in Ritee's place. But today Suju's words touched some chord of his heart. Fortuitously it made him to think about it. He came to know from Suju that both the girls are equally good looking. He listened to his intuition and when he tried to introspect, found the second girl's family would be a good prospect. They are a middle class family well settled in Mumbai. They are only two siblings and the elder brother is working in Dubai, whose marriage proposal has come for Srijesh's sister. It will be a perfect nexus of their families. Srijesh can be abstained from putting hard effort for his sister's marriage if she ties the knot with the guy settled in Dubai.

Srijesh didn't want a pie to leave Suju in this critical condition. He knew Suju lacks time; on the other hand Suju wished him luck and sent him to Bangalore. His only wish was to allow him to meet the second girl named Sophia Joseph. And very next day Srijesh took the train to Bangalore city.

25

"*O*k. We can meet by 6pm."

Sophia disconnected the call as they both decided to meet over a Saturday weekend in centrally located Church Street. She along with few of her friends was waiting outside the tea shop, each one having a lighted cigarette in hand. Srijesh called Sophia once again and gave a message of his presence near to coffee shop. Immediately she lit off the cigarette and chewed two bubble gums. Her friends left for the sake of her first date with Srijesh. Srijesh and Sophia saw and greeted each other by a gentle smile on their faces.

"So, coffee."

"Sure."

"CCD or Costa."

"Ahh . . . let's go to Hardrock café."

Srijesh could not digest the answer from Sophia. "On the very first meeting this girl is asking to go Hardrock," Srijesh talked to himself. Poor fellow does not know that Sophia has already planned for some malign tactics to get rejected. From the very first sight Srijesh knew, Sophia is not the conventional type of girl who comes to earth with a single motive to marry and then happily live ever after. She is not the kind of some typical south Indian orthodox girls. She is smart, independent, feisty girl who can intimidate any men with her lustrous communication. But if her physical beauty is concerned then she is tall, dusky, charming girl who can mould any men with her sexy looks.

"Are you sure to go Hardrock this time?" Srijesh was little surprised but considered Sophia's choice as purely indigenous. You can take a Keralite out of Kerala but you can't take Kerala out of a Keralite. Sophia proved it that instance. After one peg each, Sophia started interrogating Srijesh.

"So, what are your hobbies?" And her actual intention was to know if this fellow would be a good companion during leisure.

"Hmmm. Reading novels, travelling etc."

"And . . ."

"And . . ." Srijesh told few others but never came near to Sophia's favourite hobbies. Watching Bollywood movies and speaking in Hindi. It must be the heavy impact of film city. So in the very first test Srijesh scored zero.

After few more tricky questions, Sophia bombarded the final one. "Do you have any girlfriend or had in the past?" And her acute intention was to know if this fellow would be romantic in married life too.

Sophia made him remember Ritee for a while. He could not search any other answer than, "No." This question answer session snared him to a paradox and he miserably thought of himself, "Shame on you man. Whether groom has come to see the bride or bride has come to see the groom." And he scored one more zero.

"Look Srijesh. You might be a nice guy. You are. But I am a different type of girl and can't be compatible to you. And you won't be able to handle me if I put my conditions in front of you." Sophia tried to show her over smartness.

"What type of condition?" Srijesh asked.

"See, I want my space, freedom, my own life. I can't quit the job for the sake of family or married life in future. I might pursue to go abroad if opportunities come in my career. And last but the most important one, no kids . . . at least for the first five years of marriage."

"Okay, but I thought you will put your conditions."

"That's what I said."

Srijesh pasted an acquitted smile on his face and replied, "Sophia, whatever you said is not called condition. These are your ambitions. And ambitions are compulsory for life. Without which life will be soulless. You must be proud to yourself. Don't you think so?" For the first time Sophia saw the chivalrous Srijesh, when he answered her in a much confident way. And Sophia could give a score at least six out of ten.

"Hmmm . . . when I saw you first, I thought you must be a boring formal guy. But now I realize . . . you are not."

"But here music is so boring. Isn't it?"

"Yeah, but who cares?"

"Wait a minute." Srijesh progressed towards the stage and borrowed the guitar from the musician. He played a marvellous tune. And here he can't ever be less than ten on ten. He mesmerized everyone including Sophia. Srijesh felt regaining his charisma. He realized he has not lost his charm once he poses in Goa. He was thankful to Sophia for this evening and Sophia on the other hand had a great time with Srijesh.

They both kept in touch while staying in Bangalore. Sometimes casual meet, sms, phone calls kept them engaged and after few days Hard rock café stated juggling between CCD and Costa. Sophia realized that Srijesh won't be a bad choice if she marries him, whereas Srijesh felt Sophia will definitely help him to forget Ritee from his life. Whenever he met Sophia, he became nostalgic of his Goa days. He related himself to Sophia's blithe and fun-loving attitude. He felt, they both are like-minds and it will certainly attract each other. He once again felt the lead of a woman in a man's life.

Few more months passed and the final call from Goa came. It was the call from the hospital where Suju was undergoing for his uncured treatment. He had to rush for Goa in the cold winter to see Suju. He has already decided to bring him permanently to Bangalore. But he realized it was too late after seeing Suju in the hospital bed. Suju was counting his last breath but saved some of them to meet Srijesh. He was waiting for him, so that he can take him for the last time to their beach side house where they have spent the best phases of their lives. Before leaving the world, Suju wants to remind the impish jokes they used to play, the frivolous celebration they used to make in the house. Perhaps he has already accepted that he is sitting on the concluding part of his life.

Srijesh took him to their beach side house. He could hardly remember when he has seen tears in Suju's eyes apart from while he was drunk. But today is that omen. He has not been able to see his father in this stage but reminds of him after observing Suju. Suju lamented over him like a small child when they entered the house. It was vacant from last few days and looks filthier. Srijesh cleaned it properly and made Suju to be comfortable.

"So, did you like the girl?"

Srijesh understood his words after watching his twist of tongue rather than hearing his voice. It slithered and heavily narrowed due to pain. Today Srijesh didn't distract the conversation and said, "Yes Uncle. She is a nice girl."

"Ok, then marry her. I wish I could be present there."

"Of course you can. Very soon I will take you to Mahe," Srijesh answered the false statement though he was much aware of the truth.

"I know son. It is not possible. That is why I am telling you few things. Just promise me that you will keep my words."

Srijesh shook his head while sobbing and promised to oblige it. He patiently listened to Suju's rubbish wishes, where his every word described some abysmal determinations to live. His breath were tired of convulsion and inviting him to sleep for the longest hours. Suju every time tells, he belongs to Goa and the day he dies, his body should get buried in this soil where it can rest in peace. It can rest in peace if it gets a suitable place near to a beautiful woman's grave and savour him an aromatic taste of romance. He didn't insist Srijesh to shower some flowers over his coffin, but he will express his gratitude if two Malaysian strawberry flavoured condom packets will be allowed to dispose along with him. Suju wanted to dance in hell after death and if God sanctions, he would like to reborn as the richest playboy of Goa in his next life. Though it was madness but Srijesh sincerely performed the last rite with paramount honesty. And Suju, even while consuming his last breath, he didn't stop endowing some blessings to his beloved Srijesh. He has insisted him to open the letter only after his death, where he has written:

MY SON. I WILL NOT BE IN THE WORLD WHEN YOU READ THIS LETTER. I LOVED MY LIFE ONLY BECAUSE OF YOU AND I COULD LIVE IT LONGER ONLY FOR YOU. FEW THINGS I COULD NOT TAKE IT WITH ME AND I REQUEST YOU TO TAKE CARE OF IT PROPERLY. THERE IS SOME MONEY LEFT IN MY ACCOUNT AND THE HOUSE PROPERTY I KEPT IN MY SUITCASE. ALL ARE YOURS. ENJOY. I HAVE DECIDED TO PRESENT IT IN YOUR MARRIAGE. BUT I FAILED AS I HAVE TO LEAVE EARLY IT SEEMS. PROMISE ME. YOU WILL HAVE A GOOD LIFE AND START YOUR FAMILY SOON. AND WHENEVER YOU FEEL YOU ARE HAPPY, REMEMBER, YOUR SUJU UNCLE WILL BE SEEING YOU NEARBY.

His handwriting was dirty. But, for the first and last time, there were no spelling mistakes.

26

$\mathcal{S}$rijesh kept his promise and decided to marry Sophia. After almost a year their marriage date fixed for the month of February. Now Srijesh is a known lecturer and settled in Bangalore. Sophia's job was going well and they both approved to take their relationship to the next level. Their marriage date is finalized for February 25th in Holy Christ Church followed by reception in Town Hall. Very next day his sister's marriage is fixed with Sophia's brother.

Sophia was happy as she found a groom who is understanding in nature and doesn't interfere in her personal space. Her ever-lasting smile in reception was revealing it all. Srijesh has also accepted that Sophia is the girl and will be throughout his life. His past has to be sunk from this time onwards. He has to burn the memories of Ritee, the innocent face, the cherubic smile; he was once ready to die for. He decides to search the same innocence in Sophia and he knows he will succeed one day. And the journey he begins with a step to spend the first night with Sophia.

Srijesh's numerous attempts to refrain himself from drinking went in vain when his friends compelled him to have some scotch. But Sophia didn't mind at all as she welcomed him inside the bedroom in a sizzling posture. After discussing few mundane topics as a matter of formality they smelled the flavour of inching moment. Srijesh knew this moment will be crucial as he has never attempted with anybody. Of course in Saudi his roommates had brought few prostitutes, but he has not disrupted his chastity with anybody other than Ritee. But why is he being coerced today and what makes him think about Ritee? Today is his day and the night will be under his sole authority. He can do whatever he wants with Sophia, but time is slowly turning out to be what he can do after all.

Sitting on the couch, Sophia realized that somebody has to initiate and it will be truly special if she seduces Srijesh to begin their intimacy. She asked him to show his finger

132

ring and in process she slowly drove her fingers towards Srijesh's chest routed through the arms. The slither in his body in a form of agitation tempted Sophia to ask, "You are responding like a typical virgin." And her mild sense of humour energized Srijesh like an aphrodisiac to bully hit his testosterone. He held Sophia's arm tightly as if she challenged his masculinity. He punished her vigorously as he kissed her lips in a long succession.

"Ouch, easy, easy."

Though Sophia interrupted but she liked the wildness which reserved the pouting expression alive on her juicy lips. She slowly closed her eyes and made her racy breath intensely audible to Srijesh. And Srijesh progressed to make the first soothing kiss.

"Oh my God. It was illicit." He is still being imbibed with Ritee's thought. The more he progresses the more he feels wounded by Ritee's sensuous touch and the magical moment they have spent. He knows it is completely wrong. He should not think about the other lady while spending the very first night with his lawful wife. He felt helpless and sinful. He can't become a demon and nail Sophia in bed, keeping Ritee in his mind. Sophia's wait to receive some more kisses became impulsive and amidst these entire crux an irritating alarm bell rang when three needles touched together in the watch. It was 12 am and how rude, that cooled down their libido for a while and brought a skimpy smile on their faces.

"Shall we go to bed? It is uncomfortable here," Sophia said posing a shy smile.

She found the absence of romantic buzz in Srijesh who didn't carry her in his arms up to the flowery bed and the moment they sat on the bed, one more alarm bell rang. It was idiotic and Srijesh realized his friend's impishness, they have kept few more watches on alarm mode. Bloody idiots. He then started searching the hidden watches inside the room. He turned few of them off and by the time he returned to bed, half of his desire faltered. Without wasting any more time Sophia tried to unbutton Srijesh's shirt and guided his hands to undress her. It was quite easier as she was in a silk sari.

"I should switch off the light," Srijesh asked for permission.

"No need. It will be convenient in light. Just bring the Cap."

"What?"

"C."

"Sorry."

"Oh God. Cap, Condoms whatever."

Srijesh was stupefied as he has never thought about it neither he can get any pharmacy shop open in this time of night.

"Oh no, I haven't brought it."

"Then what were you searching there in cupboard?"

"I was searching the other watches my friends might have kept activated."

"What kind of friends, can't even gift a condom packet in friend's marriage reception." Sophia thought dispiritedly, "Ok, then proceed carefully but try to withdraw on time."

And finally one more alarm bell resonated, which was undoubtedly the most horrible amongst all. In between all these turmoil, the night became restlessly awkward for Srijesh who ejaculated prematurely while performing the duet. All thanks to these countless hindrances. Clocks are made for managing time succinctly but this time it encouraged for a total mistiming. He felt dejected.

"Don't worry. I have heard it happens during first time." Sophia tried to reassure.

Srijesh felt even more dismayed as Sophia termed him as a first—timer in this field.

"Great. You seem quite intelligent in this topic."

"Oh. Now you are trying to embarrass me. Forget today. We will complete it crisply in our honeymoon suite."

"Okay and where have you planned for?"

"Now that's a surprise. My friends have offered me a honeymoon package. It's a lovely resort I found in internet. We can have lots of fun which we can't do actively in this house."

"And where is it by the way?" Srijesh casually asked by posing a smiley face.

"Name of the resort is Blue Lagoon of . . . the . . . romantic . . . Goa." Sophia was expecting a definite exuberance in Srijesh face and hence emphasized her every words. But it turned ineffectual and on the contrary he startled.

27

 *E*ven after repeatedly questioned by Sophia, Srijesh preferred to be silent. It is not a coincidence; rather he felt it like a cruel joke spit on him. Giving a pretext of work schedule he requested to cancel the plan of Blue Lagoon. But Sophia retained her super ego and cancelled the entire plan of honeymoon itself. They returned Bangalore downheartedly.

Like thousands of working couple they tried to live a decent life, where both were having little time to cheer for each other. Five days of extensive work followed by a Saturday to cleanse the tiredness and a Sunday which usually gets occupied in upbringing the next five days plan. In between if they are fortunate to get some valuable times; they try to accommodate themselves in each other's space. Seeking a better tomorrow, they crushed their dreams of todays. Extra work hours, overtime became an integral part of daily routine and sex life acted as a lacklustre part time duty reserved for weekends. Life has never been so dull so tedious before for Sophia. A small outing, dinner a date in a month makes her so glad which used to be very common and trivial before marriage. She misses the girl's day out, the pub, parties which are turned like a day dream to her. But what kept Sophia lively is her quintessential professional life. She takes pride in working for an US MNC with a team of intelligent engineers from IITs and NITs under the guidance of a super dynamic team manager Mr. Anthony Lobo. Sophia feels lucky to be one among the team of performers in the organization. Back home she is supported equally by Srijesh. He has been like a backbone and a morale booster to Sophia. And finally the day came which brought Sophia closed by a step of her career graph. What she has put as a condition for Srijesh, it happened to be true as she got an opportunity to fly Los Angeles for a six month project. That day was surely the best day in her married life. She came early in the evening and took Srijesh for a romantic candle light dinner in a beautiful

Italian restaurant. They tasted some delicious cuisine along with a bottle of fantastic wine. Sophia still kept the secret undisclosed and waited for the night and what better time it could have been after offering few hours of steamy sex to Srijesh. It was one among few memorable nights where they played for lengthy hours and released orgasm at a time. Resting her head on Srijesh's hairy chest, she asked in a mellowed tone.

"Srijesh, will you miss me if we can't see each other for about a month or two."

"Of course, but what made you ask this question?"

"It's a surprise. Our team got a project and we are going to LA for about six months, shall I?"

"Hey, that's really great. You should."

"Are you sure?"

"Don't be stupid Sophia. It is a life time opportunity for you to explore yourself. You must go."

"Thank you Srijesh. You are the most caring husband," Sophia husked and cuddled Srijesh lips for a while before making one more request.

"This time you have to promise me that you will open a Gtalk account." She tried to be aggressive as Srijesh has never enjoyed the social networking site. After few minutes of frivolous argument, Sophia opened a Gtalk account for him and made herself as the first member of his friend's list. The maiden count of friends list continued till he knew the complete function of Gtalk. Now Sophia is in Los Angeles and their mode of communication is restricted to Gtalk except few minutes of phone call once a week.

28

That was a stormy night of Saturday and after a long time fighting with dreariness, Srijesh found a slice of thought about Ritee. He condemned it to his last visit of Goa for Suju's death ceremony. Ritee has so far become a mystery in his life but the vicarious memories are still not deterred from his mind. For the sake of fantasy, Srijesh opened his computer and tried to surf some long lost friends in Gtalk. And some detrimental efforts made him to type the name of Ritee Sarkar at the end. At least ten similar profiles appeared which caused Srijesh completely thrilled. He avidly turned on one by one and his hands began shaking the more he went into the deep. His buried memories smouldered from some corner of his heart and wished vehemently to find Ritee's contact. It kept on asking him, "Is it practically possible to extract her information." His hope got melted as he did not receive any strong clue except one more concern of encouragement, he typed Sibangini Roy. Few active profiles appeared on the screen containing some openly shared photographs and profile pictures. A similar look lady found seized in a family photograph of husband wife and two little daughters. He enlarged it. Oh God. It was hard to believe his desiccated luck. It is the same Sibangini Roy, a character was in his life and an influencer once upon a time for him. His mouth was agape with incredulity and his senses made him to stand for a while. He lighted one cigarette and puffed outside the balcony door. He started believing that he can confirm about Ritee now. Her information will get unwrapped. What exactly happened to her? Where is she? Why she didn't ever try to contact him? Why she betrayed him and never appeared in his life? Is she married to a wealthy brat and living a healthy life? How about her family? Any kids or she has become a widow? All these fatal beliefs he thrust aside against the other . . . is she alive?

It took almost a week of getting his friend's request accepted by Sibangini and finally one Sunday afternoon he fetched her in the chat box.

"Hi Sibangini, How are you? Did you remember me?"

There was no single response up to an hour followed by a cheap short hand reply, "let's chat after 11 pm tonight." Srijesh didn't turn off and impatiently waited till 11 pm when one word popped up.

"Hi."

"Hi Sibangini, how are you and where are you? I would like to speak to you urgently. Would you mind sharing your number?"

"I can't speak to you now, tell me how you are?" Sibangini replied.

Srijesh could not preserve his patience and suddenly specified the sole intention behind this chat.

"Where is Ritee?"

No reply up to an hour.

"What happened? Hey, are you there?"

No reply and it is night 1 o' clock. The more Sibangini delays giving response, the more he accumulates his broken strength. He can't listen what he doesn't want to. He prayed God and was seeking a positive outcome. And finally it blinked in his chat box.

"Why do you want to know about her? And that too, now. You are married I believe."

What stupid question is this? What he should predict now? Why Sibangini is not telling clearly about Ritee? Speculations ran rife inside his mind and he could not stop his fingers to write, *"I beg you Sibangini; I need to know where Ritee is? Why are you hiding it to me, please tell me, is she alive?"*

After a protracted silence Sibangini wrote the so called life changing truth for Srijesh. *"Yes."*

"Where is she?"

"Why do you care?"

"I want to meet her Sibangini, tell me where is she?"

"Why do you want to imbalance her personal life Srijesh? She is happy with her family." And Sibangini disconnected the chat causing Srijesh to add one more watchful night to his life. The crescent moon graced his next day evening as he found a

mail from Sibangini. He knew it was going to turn around his life, where it was paragraphed.

Hi Srijesh, Ritee lives in Sonpada village on the outskirts of Kolkata. I don't know why you are asking about Ritee now and why do you want to meet her. She is staying with her husband and a daughter in her family. Don't ever try to meet and spoil her family life. And if any point of time you meet, don't ever tell that I have informed you, bye.

Sibangini showed her notorious character even now by acting like a facilitator. Perhaps she also knows Srijesh will definitely try to meet Ritee that made her to write the last sentence. Srijesh could not hold his tears neither he could control his thoughts of poignancy as he furiously entered the store room. He removed his old suitcase which carries a small box inside. He has stored Ritee's photograph in it and prayed every day to retard any situation which could tempt him to open it. But he could not. He balanced the palpitation inside his heart when his lips allowed him to kiss the photograph. Again his mind raced towards the divine destination of his past and his desire rewound to dislodge him to the place where he has learnt to love Ritee. He cannot forgive himself if he doesn't meet her this time. Even if he doesn't meet, at least he will see her from a distance to soothe his famished heart. And if his satisfaction permits him, he will remember Ritee as his first love and never interfere in her family life. He promised himself and decided to go to Kolkata without expecting anything . . . but to see her, and that could possibly be their last meeting, he realized.

29

KOLKATA
DURING THE AUSPICIOUS DURGA PUJA.

$\mathcal{S}$rijesh stepped into the soil of Kolkata for the first time and managed to search the place Sonpada. For him a little taught Hindi by Sophia worked amazingly to communicate to the strangers and he put off in a small lodge on the outskirts. It was the same carnival of auspicious Durga Puja in West Bengal and the celebration was running everywhere. He took an early morning bath, shaved a French cut, dressed himself handsomely and went near to Puja pandal. His only wish was to meet Ritee if she would come to perform the morning puja.

And . . . after eight long years, eleven months including some countable days he saw Ritee from a little distance.

Srijesh started praising his own luck. Now he can meet Ritee whom he has lost when she was the most precious gift of his life. But unfortunately, now he can't even dare to look at her for a long time. He got a proof that day that time can separate any bonding between two people. Ritee was such an integral part of his life but now he can't think of touching her. For a fraction of time he wanted to vacuum all these long years of his life and visit the same day when he has been in search of Ritee.

He continued looking at Ritee. She looks like a typical Bengali housewife in a red colour sari. Now she bows her head while walking which implies, she has already crossed her girlhood. She gestured an acquainted smile and the slither of her face implies, she has entered her womanhood. She definitely looks more than her age. She is not concerned about her beauty anymore. Except a bindi on her forehead there are no makeup applied on her face. Her lips are dry and visible with minor wounds appear while smiling. She has lost many things but . . . her beatific smile. Not even today.

"How are you Ritee?"

"Fine . . . and you?" Ritee didn't show a stress on her face even though they met unexpectedly after these many years.

"I just came to know from . . ."

"Yeah, Sibangini told me already. Come, we stay nearby." Ritee behaved formal and invited him as a guest. And Srijesh came to know, it is due to Sibangini that helped Ritee to eradicate the probable thrill on her face. She has already got to know about Srijesh's plan of coming to Kolkata well in advance. Without asking any more question, Srijesh followed her and his main objective was to know what "We" means for Ritee.

He entered her house and saw few wall hanging photographs inside the living hall. He picked one among the collage, which was a family photograph consists of a middle aged man, a young girl and Ritee herself. He can assume they will be happy in real life too after seeing the photograph.

"She is our Meethi and her father," Ritee told while handing over the tea cup to Srijesh. He didn't seem shocked but a minute jealously cleared his way to get reflected on his face.

"Nice photo," he said even though he wanted to tell, "nice family." Nevertheless it brought a smile on Ritee's face.

"Where are they by the way?"

"Meethi is here. She is now in 12th standard. And Meethi's father lives in native and comes here in some occasions."

Srijesh was rankled by listening to the traditional wifely talk of Ritee. She is not even calling her husband by name. She is pronouncing him as Meethi's father. How romantic yet how rude for Srijesh? He sulked and was being stolen all topics of discussion with Ritee. He could not swallow the snacks offered to him. As a formality, he finished the tea and wanted to wash his hand. Ritee poured some water after guiding him to the courtyard and offered a towel. When Meethi came, she introduced Srijesh as her classmate during college days. Unlike Ritee, Meethi seems a chatty girl who exchanged few words with Srijesh and left for her friend's house afterwards.

"So, till when you are in Kolkata?" Ritee asked the most unwelcomed question for a guest.

"Till tomorrow."

"You . . . you won't see the puja reception then."

"I would love to, but some work back home. I have just come to see you and now I must leave." Srijesh realized how tough it was to tell Ritee that he actually came to meet her. Still he didn't find any cordial reflection on her face. She kept her voice devoid of emotions and Srijesh could not mount for any closeness with Ritee. He properly understood now that he should not search for any rights in Ritee's life. He kept on assuring himself and felt complacent for Ritee that she chooses her life with dignity. He is happy for her family and preferred to leave permanently from there.

And Ritee . . . how can she reserve her patience within? Srijesh is the only one whom she has loved madly. Srijesh might not have noticed but she stammered while speaking. She diverted her vision from his reach of identifying. She swallowed her words and demolished those burgeoning emotions. And when her eyes were camouflaged by tears, she rushed inside her private room. And today she didn't open her favourite window to see the endless distance of paddy fields to resemble her traumatic signs of desolation; rather she opened the opposite one, just to see Srijesh walking down the narrow lane of their populous colony.

Ritee could not digest Srijesh's intention to visit Kolkata. Has he actually come to see her? Just a mere glimpse of her and his purpose is accomplished? She felt miserable as Srijesh didn't ask for a private meeting or about her personal life. Unless he asks, how she can voluntarily divulge her past. She doesn't want to be exposed, neither has she wanted to deduce the black memories. She doesn't want to gain sympathy and termed as an opportunist. She doesn't want to defend herself else she would have told everything to Srijesh. Who Meethi is and who is Meethi's father? Under what circumstances she stayed in their house without having any relation with them. Meethi is not her daughter neither Ritee shares the relationship of a spouse with Meethi's father. During these many days of spending in their house, Ritee could have bowed to her sexual desire if Meethi's father would not be paralysed in an accident. When Ritee lost her everything during super cyclone, she along with her father was adopted by them. It is only because of their support, her father consumed a painless death crossing some years of living after being severely injured in cyclone. They also lost Meethi's mother and since then Ritee stayed with them, they never treated her like an outsider to their family. Even though as a courtesy, Ritee tried to leave their family but Meethi never allowed her to do so. Now Meethi is a reason of her living and she also can't live without her.

Sitting inside the hotel room next day morning, Srijesh's mind bubbled with hundreds of speculations regarding Ritee. How she got married to a man who might be double her age? How is it possible that her daughter entered 12th standard when she herself will be turning thirty. He realized, he will end up finding some unsolved mysteries if he continues thinking about it. These speculations should remain undisclosed. He should be thankful that his dreaded thought of losing Ritee turned futile. He at least got a chance to see her living a better life. Now he should accept himself as an unknown person to Ritee. And this is the way to construct his life and let Ritee progresses hers.

He got a knock on the door. He has already finished his morning tea and now who has come to disturb him?

"Dada, somebody has come to meet you." The hotel boy told Srijesh and rushed to serve the other customers. Srijesh doesn't know anyone in this unknown territory other than Ritee. Now who has come to meet him? He put on his shirt and glanced towards the reception area. One more time he felt betrayed by his eyes as he saw Ritee, in a Pink Sari with a handkerchief in hand, standing near to the reception door. He was greeted with a rustic smile followed by an appearance of some nameless satisfactions on her face. Today Ritee looked at Srijesh the way Srijesh wanted to see her always. She is dressed the same way what he desired from her. And she looks as beautiful as she looked once they both were together.

"What a surprise?" Srijesh showed an exclamation on his face.

"It will be an insult if you leave Kolkata without seeing the puja. Once you have shown me your place and now it is my turn. And I am sure you won't regret at all." Suddenly Ritee's voice seems filled with resilience. Today she skipped visiting with Meethi only because she wanted to show her world to Srijesh in return of those memorable days offered to her. She tried to extend the maximum courtesy in a limited budget. She booked a tanga to go inside the city. She didn't even allow Srijesh to pay for the lunch which they had in Pondybazaar puja stall. They opted for metro train while travelling the places of higher distance and during evening they spent time in front of reddish water under Howrah Bridge. She was treating Srijesh as if she wanted to repay all the debts she owed from him. And finally when she was about to finish the money borrowed from Meethi, she decided to leave. Srijesh realized this could not be their last meeting at all. After spending this date it would be impossible for him to control his feet to come here repeatedly. But it should be a mutually agreed decision. And he knows he can't say no to his obligation, if Ritee invites him. He left Kolkata with a warm heart that night.

30

$\mathcal{I}$t is not true at all that Srijesh didn't remind Sophia during his time spent with Ritee. But he can't accept it as an act of preaching his lovely wife. He is coming to meet the lady whom he knows before marriage. He can't see anything wrong in that because he doesn't want to name the relation. He has burnt it many years ago and now he poses with no claim in owning Ritee. She is just a living life and a name added to his friends list.

After an extended project work Sophia returned to Bangalore. But she was back with a projection of long lists of unachievable goals. Lavish lifestyle, lucrative earning and sky high career graph in short span of time. Perhaps her project work taught her more of psychological aspects of life, rather than technical benefits. Or was it an impact of Western culture. Srijesh never tried to dispirit her but this reluctance of Srijesh day by day expanded Sophia's aspiration. And he applied the best method for supporting his wife, which is to blindly 'obeying'. But Sophia has become unreasonably demanding nowadays. When Srijesh obeys, she demands respect. When he gives respect, she expects care. When he cares for her, she asks for love and when he loves her, she seeks unlimitedly what a healthy woman needs from her husband to fulfil the opulent desire of her craving body. Srijesh tries to give whatever he can as per his capability and strength, but Sophia now feels proud in effort of snatching her pie. And that leads to a sheer dissatisfaction in their married life. But she never realizes as her professional life started offering more than she deserves. She is cruising beyond the speed of her competitors which has created an envious environment for her inside office. She is the ace performer in her team and building certain benchmarks to chase by others. Where friends give credit to her intelligence and smartness, the foes blame it to her proximity with her boss Anthony. Who says boss cannot be friends. At least it is not accountable in Sophia's case. And she is taking the best use of it even though she shares only a platonic relationship with him. When most of her colleagues burn of jealousy and hardly accompany her, it is Anthony who gives her perfect company every time. Be it for coffee, smoking or going to restaurants occasionally. Even in some occasions he is invited for dinner to Sophia's house or sometimes for casual parties. Srijesh did not mind Anthony's introduction to his family as he started sharing a cordial relationship with him like a philanthropist. But he abhors sometimes being targeted in dinner table when Sophia and Anthony take one side to flout his banal profession. Anthony has referred him strongly to opt for few corporate sectors but Srijesh has never shown his regards to accept those offers. Sophia feels cautious and wishes the decision taken by Srijesh must not hinder her rapport with Anthony. Anthony is her idol and she believes she will succeed by following his footsteps. Srijesh on the other hand is happy as his job of lectureship appeases him, so as his personal life. He feels fortunate for having a beautiful wife, his family and friends and a special friend Ritee in his life whom he has lost once and found against destiny's will.

Unknown to Sophia, he calls Ritee few times a week over phone without anticipating any tribute from her. It is just to show his concern like a true friend. But very soon this concern of friend proliferates into a possessive concern of guardian. Once again Ritee's innocence becomes dominant encroachment to his emotions. Without intimating the actual cause to Sophia, Srijesh travels to Kolkata frequently. And Ritee also never refrains from removing her family bonding and comes to meet him with optimum delight. Every time she waits for him keeping the same alacrity in heart and felicitates him with equal zest. The moment she gets the divine notification of Srijesh arrival, she dresses herself to look appealing to his eyes. Only those few days she uses Meethi's wardrobe. During that time she prepares some sweet dish and carries it for Srijesh. And when Srijesh applauses it, she blooms in embarrassment. She feels being defrosted in his affection and celebrates every moments spent with Srijesh. She knows, she can't bring back that good old time when she used to be his beloved and now she wants to perform the same responsibilities whose opportunities she has lost a long time ago. But even in this favour, she has not overlooked the frontier of their relationship. She has taken a promise not to fall again for Srijesh and hits back when Srijesh tries to cross his brinks.

"Ritee, promise me you won't refuse it." He became sanguine and handed over the present with a delectable anxiety.

Ritee was dismayed for a while but complied with his request by wearing the necklace for few minutes. Srijesh was ecstatic after seeing her. He felt he has taken revenge to his cruel dreams where he saw Ritee without any ornaments. He can't express how lucky he feels as Ritee acknowledged his present. He feels blessed if anything he could do for Ritee and today she has accepted the most precious gift. Today also there is full moon and nobody else to interrupt them. He decided to accuse the romantic evening thereafter, which aroused his curiosity to touch Ritee. But his outlook faded when she bent her lips away from his reach.

"What happened Ritee?"

Probably he thought Ritee might accept for a kiss as she gave consent for his gift. But he failed as both of his wishes turned ephemeral when Ritee removed the necklace and handed it over.

"I can't take it Srijesh."

"But why Ritee?"

"It is a gift which normally a husband can give to his wife. It will look beautiful only at that scenario. And by this act, we are going to cheat somebody else Srijesh."

"If you believe you are cheating on your family, why do you come to meet me Ritee? Are you not completely satisfied with your husband?" And finally Srijesh asked for that answer what he was desperately seeking from Ritee. He has seen her desisting from many rituals a married Hindu woman follows. She never puts vermilion powder or wears bangles or finger rings. And her superficial apparels have certainly kept him surreptitious about the truth.

"That doesn't mean I am not satisfied with my family. But why do you come to meet me again and again Srijesh. Aren't you being faithful to your wife?"

This statement by Ritee surely stabbed the male ego inside Srijesh and for a fraction of second he wanted to punish Ritee for her sarcastic remark. For the first time they talked about their personal life but it sounded like revealing each other's deficiencies. Srijesh could remember how hard it was for him to save a substantial amount from his salary and to buy this expensive gift. And all is to achieve Ritee's hatred. This is injustice. For him it became the maiden scion of his existence, "whether Ritee has ever loved him."

And he asked repeatedly, "So you never loved me Ritee, not even now, not in Goa, not even any point of your life?"

Ritee consolidated her silence and left Srijesh persistently humiliated. Srijesh realized he is losing his self-respect, yet he stood by to his chagrin, "Tell me Ritee, have you ever loved me . . . at least for a day?" He reiterated and his words appeared with convulsion and intrigued Ritee for an instant reply. Ritee still lingered for a while and kept on testing his patience. Srijesh felt miserable and capitulated to Ritee's highness. That moment he acted like a slave and ready to face every punishment from Ritee. If she phrases anything other than a refusal, Srijesh has decided to kiss her with ardour and embrace her for life. But certainly the same was not felt by Ritee who stuck to her insensitive promise and replied, "We human don't love somebody else Srijesh. We love only ourselves. We seek protection and love our parents. When we inherit our desires we love our mates and when we grow older we become dependent to our own children and love them. I have crossed the arena and left with no strength to love you."

"Why you are saying like this Ritee? Can't you see me bleeding every second yearning for your love?" He pleaded ceaselessly.

"There is no future Srijesh. You have your wife, your own family; you must devote your time for them and allow me to live mine."

"Then why you didn't come to me that time Ritee. I thought, I lost you but you were alive. I am happy now. I can tell myself whole life that my love for you was unconditionally true. But you betrayed me."

Srijesh became indignant and left the place keeping no intention to renter Ritee's life. He decided to break all plausible relations and never tries to remind the character named Ritee ever existed in his life. But the failure of winning her love pushed him for a loveless marriage life. Now he badly feels the explosion of guilt inside and dithers to face Sophia whenever she craves for her part of physical love.

31

$\mathcal{I}$t was a black Friday in Sophia's professional life, when she heard that there are no buyers for their dream project they invested for US based financial institutions. It was not because of the quality of products they prepared but because of the dipping economy due to recession. When a blue-chip company went bankrupt, it left its vendors consists of small companies on a verge to perish completely. And they were not in a position to fight the collateral damage caused to them. Sophia's employer was one of them. Hundreds of employees got sacked having no projects left and performers like Sophia and others went on bench. The situation for them was like a suspended bureaucrat who continues having foot in two boats at a time. They seldom opt for new job and still dwindle to continue in the same place. And senior faithful managers like Anthony were fiercely searching for some new projects for their company's survival.

Though Anthony gets exasperated by Sophia's foolish questions regarding job stability, he never discourages her. He comes to her house with same enthusiasm and brings champagne for them in dinner table. They discuss about the topics of volatile market, economic failure and the future of IT related jobs. In the same place of dinner table but now Srijesh holds the key to tame them as life has taken a U-turn placing him on the driver's seat. He is highly conceited of his decision for not opting jobs referred by Anthony and Sophia. Sophia's ambition has worsened her confidence so badly for the last three months that now she is doing nothing but to wait for the judgement day. If she loses it, she must require a strong shoulder to place her head and mitigate the dampen spirits. It must be her husband's whom she underestimated one point of time when she was on her sky high career. But she doesn't know the person, who she wants to be relied on, is burning in his own world of quarrelsome desperation. He is still not able to come out as a winner in the war of

151

molesting Ritee's memories. Why he fell for a woman who sucked his life to hell. And that one question still remains an enigma to his life. "Does she ever love him?"

He didn't get it so far. But he got a flash of hope when he received the shortest letter from Ritee to his professional address.

Dear Srijesh,

*I want to meet you for the last time. If you have still some space left for me, please try to come next month 7*th*. I will be alone as Meethi is travelling to her native. In her absence, maybe I can be honest and explain the concerns raised by you.*

Please tear this letter after reading.

And she still didn't write her name.

Srijesh ripped this letter into miniscule after reading it and didn't get lure by Ritee's invitation. He decided to stay with Sophia as she needed moral supports mandatorily. From past few days Sophia was trying her best practices to be an obedient wife. But that day Srijesh realized it was too much. May be he has never thought of this kind of miserable situation to come for an ambitious girl like Sophia. When he came late and removed his shoes while sitting on the sofa, Sophia took it and placed on the stand.

"Just fresh n up. I will bring tea."

The moment he came out of the washroom, Sophia was ready with the teacup.

"What shall I prepare?" She asked while serving the tea.

"As your wish or shall I bring something from restaurant. You tell." Srijesh said.

"No, don't bother. I will prepare your favourite fish curry today."

"Fine, then let me go to the market. I will search some good fish today."

"No need. I have brought it already."

For the first time in history, Sophia went personally to the stinky fish market and bought some fish for Srijesh.

Srijesh has never envisaged this avatar of Sophia, which jabbed him to ask.

"Are you okay?"

"Yeah, why?"

"No, simply I asked."

"But you look tired. I will give you a massage in bed tonight." It is once in a blue moon Sophia initiates the cosiness. And today she is prepared to do that.

"Sophia. You don't have to do all this. Just relax."

Sophia hugged him but her dull face didn't entice Srijesh. He brought her consciousness by detaching himself from her extended arms. Relaxing in the bedroom Sophia started a conversation, which Srijesh has never expected that it could change his decision further.

"How is your work going on?" Sophia asked.

"Yeah it is fine. I am getting few projects from some NGOs too."

"Oh. That sounds good."

After few minutes of silence Srijesh resumed the conversation.

"Sophia, I might have to go few places to complete the projects."

"Okay. But where?"

"I have to visit the north east region followed by the east . . . probably to end in . . . Kolkata." Srijesh released a heavy breath while naming Kolkata, "but it is ok if you insist, I will cancel my plan."

"No, no. Don't worry about me. Anyways, I don't have to go to office. I will relax for few days. By the way, when you have to leave?"

"This Saturday evening."

And he left Sophia when she needed him the most. Sophia didn't blame him as she knows, how much important his job is for their family's survival. But now every moment Sophia lives in phobic inwardly. The ill consternation of losing her job harasses her and there is no one other than Anthony for seeking some optimism. But nowadays Anthony also tries to avoid Sophia, which hurts her badly. Next week the circular is supposed to come for the list of retained employees. And on that Sunday afternoon a message blinked in Sophia's mobile.

"*Every time there is a beautiful morning after the thunderous night. Don't worry, everything will be fine.*" It was from Anthony.

In return Sophia replied, "Just shut up. Don't put salt in my wound."

She was desperate to speak to Anthony from a long time. She trusts him the most and believes his words blindly. Last few days were really irascible for her as she was not able to speak to him properly and what she has done today. She ridiculed him. Anthony doesn't deserve this last message. She kept on thinking and finally called him to seek an apology.

"It is so nice that you call Sophia," Anthony immediately answered after pressing the voice button.

"I am sorry," Sophia told in a low tone.

"For what?"

"For my last message." Sophia behaved like an adorable kid and her voice signalled childish to Anthony.

"It is okay, but why you seem so dull."

"As if you don't know anything. I am not as lucky as you Anthony."

"Hey . . . are you alone? Can we meet somewhere?"

"Yeah. As you wish."

"I will be waiting for you in Forum. Let's catch up by 6 in the evening." Anthony suggested and thereafter disconnected the call. That was the first time in life Sophia reached before time to the meeting point. By seeing her, Anthony realized that he has to bear her emotional tortures. They entered the coffee shop and Anthony ordered two cups of cold frappe and a dark chocolate fantasy to assist Sophia to cool down her head first.

"Now tell me, why you are not that typical Sophia whom we know?"

"What do you mean?"

"I mean just look at you. Where is that jovial, dominant and ambitious girl Sophia?"

"Because that ambition is crushed and she doesn't know how to overcome the failure." She looked completely demoralized.

"You are not a failure, believe me you are not," Anthony said.

"Of course I am. My work experience is obsolete. I am not even drawing one third of my actual salary. My friends are now zooming in their respective jobs and ex colleagues whoever left the job have now surpassed me in their current offers." Sophia's frustration became her ambassador in communicating as she looked completely admonished. The cold frappe and chocolate fantasy changed their suitable forms being unutilized.

"Sophia, this is not the end for you remember. It is just you have begun your career. You have a long way to go. I also referred you few places where you could have reshaped your career. But you decided to stay here. Now as you have already stayed, it is just a matter of one day. And . . ."

"And the verdict will be out. I will be thrown out of the company. Door shut permanently. I didn't quit because I didn't want to. I loved this company and my job. If I move on now, I don't know how fair I may come to the new employer's expectation. And moreover you will not be there; I stuck here because of you . . ."

Anthony hanged on for a second and put down the frappe from his mouth. What Sophia meant about her last sentence. He looked at Sophia to read her mysterious eyes.

"And your support." An intelligent Sophia completed the sentence so as to void Anthony's remarks for her but she could not stop to release a drop of tear during the effort in swallowing the remaining words. Sophia badly needed somebody to be a companion in sharing her bereft. Anthony proved himself as her best friend that day and continuously motivated her.

"Sophia, there are very few who achieve this much success in their initial stage of career. And you are one of them. It is just bad luck. But time will never be the same, you know that. I have closely observed you. You have that calibre in you. Soon you are going to be on top. Mark my words."

Sophia didn't interrupt as she badly needed this appreciation and she wanted to listen more and more from Anthony. But to receive those, she has to run the conversation.

"I can't achieve anything beyond this Anthony. You can't understand my dream, my vision. A middle class girl like me pursues dreams with dedication. And now I don't want to go back. For you, my reaction might sound ludicrous. You earn a six digit salary, you drive a Honda Accord. You have got your own house in Posh Bangalore. You can never feel the grief."

Anthony smiled and asked, "Have you ever tried to know about my family Sophia?"

And Sophia looked clueless.

"Do you have some of your precious time for today evening?"

Sophia's reaction was still unchanged.

Anthony took her for a long drive to the posh yet the serene part of Bangalore, where he lives. That was an evening belonged to the breezy rain. The wiper started cleaning the front glass and Sophia wished if something could wipe out her sorrows as well. The headlight of the car dimmed as they reached the front gate of the compound. A security guard opened the gate and it took again a while roaming inside the campus and reach out his house located at the corner most part. Sophia's notion for Anthony solidified as she looked his plush house. They got drenched a little while entering the main door after parking the car. Ritee could hear the echo produced by her stiletto while entering the living hall.

Anthony brought a wine bottle from his private bar and offered one glass to Sophia. They sat on the pent house and slowly sipped the wine glass to empty. She found few erotic wall paintings in the house and got fascinated by its vibes. Her mind started licking so many questions about Anthony and what made him to bring her here. But she herself remained unanswered for what made her to come along with him. Showing a beautiful painting of a gorgeous lady she asked, "She looks beautiful in painting, how beautiful she would be in real life?"

"Of course she was . . ."

"Really, who is she?"

"My late wife. I lost her three years ago."

It totally numbed Sophia's senses for a while. "I am sorry Anthony." She came close to him and held his hands to console.

"It is ok Sophia."

156

Holding her hands he resumed, "Everyone tells I am rich, introvert and a self-centred person. But it is not true Sophia. I have lost many things which changed me entirely. And I wish I could be lucky like you. You are smart, intelligent and a brave girl Sophia. And a brave girl like you never runs behind luck, you deserve that all."

Sophia closed her eyes and two drops of tears fell on Anthony's palm. She always respects Anthony and venerates his personality. He is a tall, dark and handsome man from appearance, but kind and gentle from his behaviour. Any beautiful girl can die for him to obtain his love in return. She would be in seventh heaven if she would have found a man like Anthony. She continued weeping and her damp eyes didn't dare to look at him. She hugged him and her face could only manage to fall on his chest. Anthony applied all his efforts to calm her down, still his persuasiveness failed that day, but his action did not. He caressed her hair and slowly whispered to her ears.

"Shhh . . . Calm down, calm down darling," he conveyed few more affectionate words for Sophia to lure her inclination. But at that time Sophia hardly bothered for words. She needed a person to feel, to be protected, to be cared and to be loved. And all she was receiving from that person who is not authorized to give the same. She prayed God for not to count as a sin, if she gets defeated by the act of infidelity for the time being. She would have considered that as the most sensuous gift if Anthony destroys her on the bed. But Anthony misread Sophia's untamed intention. Probably he was more protective towards his own limitations and does not want to lose a friend like Sophia at the cost of few minutes of physical satisfaction. He wanted to kiss her cheek to show his affection, he wanted to kiss her eyes to soak the tears, but he kissed her forehead, just to show how much he cares for her being a true friend. Sophia's belief and respect for Anthony got robustly elevated when she was brought back to her house purely unblemished.

For thousand times Anthony would have thought but kept unspoken, "I love you Sophia, please spend tonight with me."

And Sophia could not stop ruminating the whole night, "Oh God. Why didn't I get a chance to meet Anthony before my marriage?"

32

For a long and impetuous wait of two days, certainly Srijesh has not come to Kolkata. And this time he is not enjoying at all. It is Ritee's call after all and he has to halt his job and most importantly his family to be able to come here. She should respect her invitation. Whenever Srijesh tries to streamline his mind towards Sophia, why Ritee incites him to move the wrong steps? And why is he continuously gets provoked? Is this an extraordinary perceptive relationship with Ritee or a frenetic desire to receive her love?

One call from Ritee came and all noxious thoughts of the last two days vanished. What strength she pursues which pulls him to suffocation and gives penchant power to stir up his ill wills.

"Please wait for today. Meethi and her father are leaving tonight." Ritee disconnected the call, what she managed to make it in the morning. And Srijesh's wait for meeting Ritee turned more violent and undisciplined.

And again she called in the late evening. "Yeah they left now; I can meet you tomorrow morning. I will wait for you near the lake."

"Ritee, why can't we meet now?" Srijesh asked.

"This is not the right time Srijesh. And also it is going to be late evening."

"Just for two minutes. Please," he begged.

"No . . . please understand."

"I can't wait. I am coming. Shall I?"

"I don't know." And Ritee disconnected the call once again.

Srijesh realized that he can't defy anymore. Ritee would not have informed continually, if she is not yearning to meet him. Oh God. How can he misinterpret? In this time of night, if Ritee is updating about her loneliness, her indication is lucid. Yes, she wants to meet. Moreover she told the last sentence. "I don't know." What she intended. Certainly she has not expressed her denial. But whether the dark cloud will be a demon to obstruct his way leading to Ritee's house? He didn't care neither he was scared of anything. In the midnight he left the hotel room and progressed towards Ritee's house. Even if rain started heavily in presence of merciless wind, he didn't care at all. He knocked the door sufficiently harder and confirmed his presence to Ritee. He hurt his finger as well in the tiny vision of dark while opening the Iron gate.

"Ritee . . . Ritee." He called in a low and raspy voice.

"Is it you Srijesh?" She asked in a scary tone.

"Yes. Please open the door," Srijesh replied shamelessly.

"Oh my God. Are you mad?" Ritee pulled him inside the house and locked the door.

"You are completely drenched Srijesh. Why you didn't wait till tomorrow?" Ritee saw him shivering badly.

"Not any more Ritee. I could not wait because I have to say . . ."

"Entire night is there to discuss Srijesh, please change your shirt, else you might fall sick."

Ritee made him to sit on the chair. Bending her knee down, she helped him to unbutton his shirt and brought a towel to mop his body. She didn't feel embarrassed as if she has a hankering to do so. Perhaps she knew Srijesh would come to her that night at any cost. She boiled a glass of milk and offered it to Srijesh after putting some turmeric in it. And finally she gave some clothes and showed him the place to change. There was no current inside the house due to heavy rain and that made her to light few dim candles and the lantern. Realizing Srijesh must be hungry; she entered inside the kitchen after taking his permission and started preparing some food. Srijesh was starving to speak to Ritee but the intensity of rain didn't slow down at all. It might have ceased his wish to speak but it shoved his flames of passion closer to Ritee. And Ritee on the other hand tumbled in excitement when she heard Srijesh footsteps neared towards her. She felt the scratching of his vicious finger nail when Srijesh caressed her hair and formed a space on her neck. He whisked her ear and fingered her back for a while, leaving Ritee to stop her work. He brushed his fingers from her neck to waist resulting Ritee to close her eyes and squirm longer. After these many years also Ritee's back is so slender that even a little elevation of her hips looks so voluptuous and the curves sexier than ever.

"Please let me cook Srijesh." She should have opened the eyes while saying as her voice fell weak and was not at all opposing.

Srijesh enfolded her waist to turn her around. He looked at her face and his mind established the fact that today Ritee's impassive face has almost turned like of an adulteress and she has thrown her virginal shyness to the dust.

"Look at me Ritee."

"Huh . . ." Her voice sounded drastically low compared to her breath.

A kiss on her eyes made her to face Srijesh. Those looked fearful that they might see her demolition today. Srijesh rubbed her face with the help of the tip of his tongue and ended up touching her silky lips. It was easier for him to hold his breath than to control the feisty movement of his lips. He kissed Ritee ferociously as if he would like to devour the entire flesh of her mouth. And when Ritee's breath went out of stock, she fell on his arms and whirled the sharpest fondle to his back. Srijesh slowly progressed to touch all the scanty parts of her body and followed with numerous kisses all over. In quaking hands they both helped to undress each other completely. Srijesh lifted Ritee and searched for the appropriate place. And when he behaved aimlessly, Ritee guided him by pointing the finger towards her special room.

"Take me to the corner most room Srijesh."

He placed Ritee to recline on her bed and slept beside her thighs. He again started caressing her breasts as slow as possible which compelled Ritee to fetch his fingers and suck a little. She made his fingers wet and slowly guided those to touch her groin. She moaned his name in temptation and when it turned unconquerable, she invited him to suckle her nipples. She felt a poison being run inside each of her nerves and felt sedated when Srijesh licked her bust.

"Oh Srijesh, I love you."

"I love you too Ritee."

His moves were passionate and unbearable, when he came inside Ritee. Those were piercing and having no compassion towards the pain inside her flesh. Her groan got suppressed due to the high velocity of raindrops. She cried further and her recklessness implied that she has never felt this pleasure before and restored herself exclusively for this night. They moved swiftly for long hours on the bed complimenting each other's promiscuity until they conclude their satisfactions. And finally when they climaxed, the orgasm felt in Ritee's body slowly shifted its form and overflowed as a tear of joy from her eyes. She invited Srijesh to rest his head on her bosom.

The afterglow of this delicious intimacy prospered them to relax for a long time on the bed. Srijesh didn't wish at all to get detached from Ritee's body and clasped her badly. So did Ritee who felt the supreme beatitude, when she hid herself on Srijesh's chest and enjoyed the aroma of his hard working sweat. After many years of celibacy, she is finally rewarded with a man's flesh to get fused. She didn't feel embarrassed lying nude with Srijesh, rather she felt grateful to him. She felt grateful that Srijesh gifted her immense contentment a young lady prays for and came into tears by realizing she still poses the same scale of desire of a healthy woman. She was thanking Srijesh millions of times interiorly for making it possible.

When Srijesh was relaxing on the bed, she came out of the room and lighted the subdued lantern and few more candles one after another. She wrapped herself with a small cloth, which could only cover her private parts transparently, and went to the kitchen room. When it was late night, she woke up Srijesh and offered him some food which she managed to prepare during this interval.

"Srijesh, please have something. You must be hungry." But Srijesh had just now, what he was starving for.

"What about you."

And Ritee shook her head to deny. "I am fine. You please have." She gave a skimpy smile and continuously observed Srijesh taking food. And Srijesh fed her a bite by his own hand. How silent, how simple a life can be, they fathomed.

Away from any bonding, any rituals, they acquired solace in each other's presence. And then Srijesh decided, "It is the right time to represent the gift." He is precise now that Ritee won't decline it.

"Srijesh, I will accept this for one condition."

"What?"

"Will you stay with me permanently leaving your wife?"

Srijesh was not amazed at all. In these many years of experience, he has at least learnt something about female psyche. He brought a smile on his face and asked Ritee, "Why are you playing with me Ritee. Even you are having your own family. Can you leave them and stay with me forever."

"They are not my family Srijesh. Neither Meethi is my daughter nor am I married to her father. Now would you change your decision?" Ritee replied posting an audacious smile. She knew, Srijesh's speculation about her got clarified. But Srijesh's silence explained what she has predicted already. Srijesh can't be her at any point of time in this life. She is not hurt for what practically is not possible. And now Srijesh has to actualise his self-esteem.

"I know Srijesh. You love me a lot. But time has transformed our relationship into a fragile one. And the relation whose root is made of fear and reproach, it will not survive. I saw your wife's photograph. I am sorry that I found it in your pocket while ironing your trouser. You both look pretty as a couple. And I can't forgive myself if ever I come in between. Neither can I leave Meethi and her family in future. The life of mine is nothing . . . but a donation from them."

Ritee knew she is telling something else. For this she has not invited Srijesh. But to tell the cremated truth, "Why she chose not to contact Srijesh at that time, when the world fell apart on her." A truth what she has coveted inside her? But how can she tell it to Srijesh, which she can't tell to herself even? She chose to be dumb again.

Srijesh didn't want to argue as he presumed what Ritee meant to say. She still cares for him and prays for his blissful future. And that is possible with his family, his wife Sophia. He admired Ritee and realized there is no point to defend him by justifying his love for her. He can bequeath his life for her sake. He prayed God that night, "If I ever get a life in this world, just send me for Ritee." It was that time of night which meant a sacred moment for them. They both didn't sleep knowing that they will not see each other in future. For the last time they reminisced about their days of togetherness. Those seven nights spent in Goa which have shown them their first phrase of attraction and taught them about their reasons of living, unconditional love for each other.

Srijesh didn't wait till morning. He didn't wait for the sun light to appear and expose Ritee in their society for spending a night with him. He blessed Ritee and for one last time kissed her forehead. He left the place without looking at her for a long time, as he can't see her weeping. While coming back, he chose to come by train. He wanted to see those places which had snatched Ritee from him. The places, which had turned deserted once, are now blossomed with new trees, new flowers and all together some new lives. In these many years they have grown up and certainly surpassed him. He must learn that life moves on if he steps by marching with time. And he decided to actually move on now. He decided to go back to Sophia and give her a future that she deserves. He is stupid that he ignored her. He is cruel that he left her when she needed him and he is a loser that he didn't respect her feelings. He wants to apologize each day of his forthcoming life and love her forever. And he remembered what he has promised to God once. He remembered what he has promised in his marriage. He will respect her and will be faithful to her in good or bad times, in sickness or in good health till he is alive.

He felt his arrival like a king is coming back to meet his queen after the war victory. He arrived at Bangalore city in the early morning. Just to surprise Sophia, he has not informed about his home coming. As per their last communication, Sophia must be expecting him next week. He is curious to see her reaction. From station he bought a buckeye of fresh roses sprinkled with some vanilla perfume. He decided to give her a tight hug when they meet. He wants to laugh if she gets irritated. He has decided, from now on, he will cook one time meal. If Sophia prefers, he will give her a massage every day. No matter he understands or not, he will watch Hindi movies. He will go for shopping as many times as possible and will become the most caring husband. He planned for a new beginning of life with his lovely wife Sophia.

He requested the taxi driver not to press honk near to his house. In fact he stepped out of the taxi by a little distance from his house. Sophia sleeps late and if she is still sleeping now, he will kiss her eyelid. He must not press the calling bell to irritate her. He took out the spare key from his wallet and slowly opened the door. He was forced to smile by looking at the abrupt condition of the house and more over by seeing Sophia's wardrobe. Her favourite white top and blue jeans are thrown somewhere along with a pair of underwear. She has thrown one stiletto on the couch and another one to the different corner of the living room. One wine glass has fallen down on the dining table. Cushions from Sofa are resting on the floor and carpets along with chairs are totally disordered. He decided to clean the mess and allow Sophia to take rest for today. He kissed the flower buckeye and approached towards the bedroom. He tried to slowly open the door by taking precaution to avoid the sound produced, and then . . . he . . . saw . . . the terrible, insane and the ugliest face of curse in front of his eyes. He was not ready to believe it. He could not demarcate, whether he is in real life or in dream. His body trembled and began to startle. His eyes turned red in fear and body sweat even in the time of early morning. Roses fell down from his hand on the floor and he ran vehemently out of the house. He slapped himself harder and harder to reconfirm, "Am I in real life." He wanted to cry, he wanted to scream and he wanted to kill himself when he faced the deserving revenge for his crimes. He felt being axed when he saw his beautiful wife Sophia has slept with her friend Anthony, and Anthony has used and plucked everything from his life. His house, his bed and his wife. He wished he would have turned blind when he saw Sophia sleeping peacefully in Anthony's arms. But what he didn't see was even more dreaded than his imaginations. He should thank God for not posting him last night. Else he would have seen what his house witnessed as the most romantic night ever. But he should not forget one thing, the entire act was consensual.

It was last evening when Sophia got the biggest surprise of her life. Her employer not only retained her in present job but also they are sending her team for a two year contract project in a Singapore based MNC. And it was all possible because of the man of the moment Mr. Anthony, who begged this high profile project which not only gives immense profit to his company but it empowered him to be the most respected person in Sophia's eyes. That evening they caroused the moment in a night club. For the first time she went to the dance floor with Anthony and her body sprinted to its tune. Her joy was travelling on the upper level of sky and her heart was planting cookies inside. She couldn't stop herself of getting boozed and felt the muscular arms of Anthony when they danced together. And when Anthony dropped Sophia in her house, for the first time she couldn't say good night but kept the door open for some time and inveigled him to her house. After a long time they found themselves alone in living room and Sophia cheered two wine glasses. They couldn't realize when this luscious wine acted like a love potion that brought them closer and sealed with a ravenous kiss. Many a times they both thought to stop somewhere but they could not do it simultaneously. Sophia wanted to obey every fantasized postures of Anthony and one by one she performed those diligently. They groped each other madly and disordered every decoration of the house by rashly moving their peckish bodies. She flung her stilettos in a supreme hurry to consume maximum pulses in love making. She threw all the cushions which disallowed her to straddle on the couch to kiss Anthony voraciously. And sitting on his lap when she unashamedly started stripping her favourite white top, Anthony held her hand and said, "Stop Sophia."

Sophia was scared, whether she committed something against his wish?

"What happened?" She asked.

"Allow me dear."

These three words made Sophia tingle in her profound excitement and she flaunted herself courageously. Anthony took the privilege of removing her dresses and slowly untied her lacy undergarments. He has achieved absolute celibacy till date in the loving memories of his wife but in accordance his zest has turned into a deadly volcano. And when he saw the svelte Sophia completely naked; he injected into her and exploded it to dispatch her to the seventh heaven. They spent a restless night and could not bring sleep until morning.

33

From that unforgettable night Sophia and Srijesh are not staying together. Sophia has relocated to her friend's house knowing it is impossible to face Srijesh after that incident. The fallen roses inside her house proved that she was caught by Srijesh. But certainly this is not the only reason of their separation. They are separated from a way back when they both have disvalued each other. Just for the sake of their marriage they tried to cope up obeying their family's sanctity and the norms of their society. But that night made them realized that they are not made for each other. The fear of exposing has prevented them to meet and the support of solitude has prohibited them to reconstruct their relationship.

That was Srijesh's last day in Bangalore after receiving the letter of divorce from Sophia. He always knew that Sophia is not the kind of girl who waits for opportunities. She can snatch it and rewrite the happiness in her life. And now as per the promise he has taken once, he must oblige it. He knows he is not the one Sophia deserves, but a successful man like Anthony.

Srijesh had to come back to Bangalore once again to complete the last formality. It was the hearing of their divorce. Their marriage got officially over today which was personally ended from a long back. They both signed the final letter and like thousands of unhappy married couples they mend ways to progress each other's life. And it was Sophia who took the first step and Srijesh came to know after receiving the invitation card.

Anthony weds Sophia.

Without Sophia's knowledge, Anthony personally travelled to Mahe to invite him for their wedding. Srijesh got his dead brain when he saw Anthony. He thought inwardly, "Whether Anthony is trying to show off his greatness or wants to show some respite to the man, his wannabe bride was once married to." But his false notion about Anthony proved wrong followed by his decision to avoid their marriage after hearing the courteous remarks from him.

"You are a nice person Srijesh, and I don't want Sophia to remember you the way she is deceived by. This marriage had not been possible if you would not have resolved it amicably. We should be truly grateful to your conciliatory effort. But moreover, we will be happy if you could attend the marriage and bless us. No family members are joining from her side Srijesh, you know that. She is really . . . really alone. We tried to convince everybody. But we could not. And you are like a family to her Srijesh. Very soon we are leaving for Singapore after marriage. Please try to come."

Srijesh could not say anything for the time being but could read his loyal eyes. How wrong he was in judging a person like Anthony? He has been envious to this person's success and jealous for his luck. He has stolen his beautiful wife and completely defeated him in the race of life. But he realized he must be thankful to him. Any person in Anthony's place could have taken the ugliest advantage from Sophia throughout her life. He could have lifelong pursued the wildest desire of a man, "To get fornicated." But he is not a rascal. He is giving a name to their relationship. The biggest name called marriage, what Srijesh personally has never understood.

The whole realization procures him a little boost to open the invitation card, but his eyes were caught at the bottom where the name of the venue was mentioned. Cathedral Church, Kolva, Goa. He knew he can never be released from his past even though he tries. And now he wants to face all the problems once he has run out from. He decided to attend Sophia's marriage and most importantly to visit his sacred place Goa.

PRESENT DAYS: GOA

*H*e has not been able to enter Goa beyond Suju's graveyard. But now he decides to visit all the places where he has lived once. He wants to feel the panache and would like to see the glitter of those places. He got news last month that his good old friend Chotu has come back to Goa along with his family. His own family consists of his wife and a child.

Srijesh could not believe, even after these many years of gap, he still feels the bubbles inside his heart by seeing this place. It still pounds faster and his excitements flourish with same proportion when he steps onto this soil. He smells harder and feels the known air in his breath. He is still passionate to plunge into the beach water and throw his hand inside. He is happy that at least this place on earth has never changed its attitude and welcomes him the same way it used to do many years ago . . . neither its people. And as expected Chotu comes to Margaon Station to receive him and even now he calls him with same enthusiasm.

"BHAIYAA . . ."

His voice sounds muscular. The juvenile face has turned into a young man and his personality is changed with maturity. He is like a household name in South Goa now and he reminds of Suju, the way he markets himself to everybody. With his own effort and hard work, he is now a proud owner of a tea shop and a self-sufficient family of three, his wife, his little son and himself. Looking at his family, Srijesh realizes the importance of small happiness in life. Even though he objects, Chotu invites him to his own house for staying and escorts him like a member of his family. He reminds Srijesh their grace and support towards him. And he is indebted to them. Srijesh gets surprised by looking at Chotu's wife. She is second time pregnant even though the first child has not stopped breast feeding. And then Srijesh looks at Chotu from his head to toe.

"Don't be surprised Bhaiya, you know my stamina."

"Ok, otherwise I thought condoms are coming of cheaper qualities nowadays."

"No doubt, but for testing also you need to have more stamina." Chotu is not changed at all. He is still the disciple of Suju's carnivorous philosophies. They madly laugh and Srijesh feels nostalgic of the past. They finish the dinner on time but stay awake for long hours in the night having drinks together.

"By the way chotu, how come you won Mangalorean's second daughter man?"

"Bhaiya, I realized if I marry the younger one, I can't do anything with the elder one, but if I marry the elder one I can touch the younger one too." And they laugh even noisier this time.

"Jokes apart Bhaiya, I am happy now with my family. And I saw you today; I am the happiest person in the world."

PRESENT DAYS:
THE WEDDING DATE

*S*ophia and Anthony are going to be second time lucky today. Among few friends and relatives they have arranged the marriage function in Cathedral Church. Anthony is happy but he knows the same is not true for Sophia. She has taken the boldest decision of her life and nobody from her family is backing her. Anthony has tried to invite everyone but they kept uninvolved from this marriage. But one person, whom they are not expecting at all, arrives at the function on time.

"Thank you very much for coming Srijesh. Sophia will be very happy. Come inside, let's meet her once. Come, come."

Srijesh is scared. He himself has taken the boldest decision of his life by coming to his ex-wife's marriage and how will he face her? What is he going to say and how Sophia is going to react? But Anthony escorts him like an esteem guest is being welcomed to meet his bride. Probably he believes that Sophia will be delighted to see at least one family member. And that is Srijesh who has come, just to oblige his request.

"Hey Sophia, I have got a surprise for you. Look who has come?"

And after a long time they both face each other. Sophia bothers to come out of the bridal chair to greet Srijesh, which she has not done to any of the guests while introducing. She can't stop her tear neither can Srijesh. They both want to confess numerous times to each other but they restore their incoherent voice in some corner of their hearts. Srijesh feels obligated to Anthony as he has always taken care of Sophia like a true friend. And even today he is concerned for the smallest happiness of her life. Anthony is giving her a future what she has aspired for. He is taking her to abroad and will fulfil her dreams. Srijesh feels thankful to God for making Anthony as the life partner of Sophia. He blends both of their hands and says, "I know, you both will be the best couple. God bless you." And he leaves from there.

"Aren't you staying for the marriage?"

"Why not, I am still a family," Srijesh replies with a smile.

Friends assemble inside the church and Srijesh standing at the corner most place of the church gives blessings to the newlywed couple. He realizes how difficult it would have been if he loved Sophia for a day at least. But he has not. Truly, wholeheartedly, he has never done it. It is not Sophia, but he has betrayed her in every single moment of their married life. If he asks himself, he gets only one answer about whom he has loved. It is Ritee, Ritee and nobody else. And life has placed him in that junction where he can't be with her ever. He comes out of the church and feels a promising bite of sunray. It is a ray of encouragement, a ray of motivation and a ray of hope. He should thank all and begin his life with a new way. He knows, his life can never be complete without Ritee but it can't be empty either. Because even today he can see Srijesh and Ritee standing at the corner most part of the church and he is teaching her to say, "Amen."

Dear Ritee,

    You are the most precious gift of my life and loving you is my ultimate salvation. I will keep the promise for my entire life and will not appear in front of you again. Once you have told a relation can't be sustained in fear and reproach. I lost many of them, but I still feel myself as the richest person in the world. You know why, I have left with plenty of your memories in me and it will remain throughout my life. If I were at your place, I would have surrendered a long back. I have already had when I came to see you and your life was turmoil in disaster. But every moment your memories kept me alive. I would have never understood your love for me, if I haven't met you last time. Thank you for framing my love within you.

    And now time has come to go back to my native, my family where I belong to.

Yours
Srijesh.

    Srijesh could never send this letter and keeps it with him always. And he believes this decision will be respected by Ritee as well. It is never easy for both of them to shatter their family bonding and they don't want to feel small by circumscribing their relation only in bed. They realize it will be easier to spend their respective lives in each other's memories rather than meeting for few minutes of satisfaction by hiding themselves from this hypocritical society.

    Srijesh leaves for Mahe and never tries to contact Ritee.

    And . . . Ritee,

    Sitting in her personal room while looking at the same paddy fields, talks to her hidden truth whenever she finds the grievous nights attacked by some cold blooded clouds along with the heartless wind which reminds about that day which took everything from her . . . everything.

1999, COASTAL ORISSA & WEST BENGAL BORDER THE SUPER CYCLONE

Her Family, who have never come together, came under one roof to combat the so far invincible cyclone. Her stepmother always counts her family as five members. And even that day it was five, but there was a new face included in it, Ritee's. When they coalesced, Mother found her young boy missing. Her ragging mouth smacked her husband and sent him off from the house in search of their little son. For the first time Ritee saw the possessive rage of a mother for her child, who was ready to sacrifice her husband for the sake of it. She went crazy and behaved like a beast to other family members. She was crying blood and in no mood to be pacified. So did the father, he searched madly sprinting inside the mango groove, the deserted rice field and the graveyards but returned despondently. And then he saw his house was about to be perished like an earthworm inside the soil. He cried everybody but could not search anyone other than an abject voice which stroked his core.

"Baba . . . Baba . . ." It was Ritee's.

She was shuddering from head to toe and cornered herself under the broken furniture. Father tried to come near but he had to uplift the wooden beam which obstructed his way on the courtyard. And when he applied his muscles, found every other member strangled in it and lying dead. Pressing his emotions, he took the option of coming towards Ritee and rescued her. But under his hard effort, he hurt his legs badly and found it completely diluted when it got buried inside the muddy water.

"Baba . . . careful," Ritee cried.

"Beta, don't worry about me, you leave from here, leave . . ." His tone was commanding.

But where Ritee could go? It was complete dark everywhere. It was raining at monstrous force. She walked few steps but fell down due to lack of energy. She hasn't had food or fresh water from yesterday. And she was left with no choice but . . . to pray.

"Dear God, please send your angels and save us." And she fell down on earth.

But miracle happened. From nowhere two healthy men appeared there. They were speaking in a different language which Ritee could not make out. She could hardly open her eyes. But in a fainted vision she saw them offering some water. And she got the confirmation that her God has sent those people for her sake. They even saved her father and brought him from the destroyed house in a handicapped stretcher. The rain was not at all getting tired and in consequence her father started suffering from high fever. He had hurt both his legs and was not able to stand; neither could he open his eyes in convulsion. He would have surely died if he would not have been saved by the two men. And Ritee named them "Angels" for their act of virtue.

Ritee marginally got an idea from their speaking accent that they both are sailors and out of them one is like a doctor too. They were vehemently searching their vehicle where they have stored some food for journey. And when they found it, they started having some milk and bread. Ritee's father was in a dead state of mind and a senseless body. He was on a threshold to die. They didn't offer any food or milk to Ritee. Perhaps it was not sufficient. They all had lost their ways and impatiently waited for this pernicious climate to calm down. And after some time of disappointments, the sailors started finding their own way leaving Ritee and her father alone in that place. Ritee pleaded for her father's life and requested them not to leave her alone. And she pleaded for some milk too, if not, some water or food. But out of those two sailors one behaved in an insolent way. Without offering the milk bottle, he sprinkled it on Ritee's face. He wasted half of the bottle in littering it on her neck. And when few streams of milk entered through her chest, he looked her like an absolute pervert. And that moment Ritee realized that they are no longer the angels. They pose the equivalent power of Devils of getting aroused even in this fearsome moment. She wanted to flee from there but rusted her feet knowing she can't take her father. She wanted to fight with them to snatch the food but suppressed her anger knowing she might get killed. And Ritee named them "Devils" for their act of sin.

But they were neither of those. They made a deal, "The deal of give and take." They took Ritee and her father and delivered them safely to the rehab centre, from where Ritee resumed her life. But, it was certainly not at the cost of their virtue. They stopped their vehicle in between when they found a secluded house nearby. They offered her good amount of food and milk and when she moved out deriving some stamina, they reminded her deal, "The deal of give and take," where Ritee had to give her everything to secure her life and they took her body to destroy the soul with in.

They meant only business. Because . . .

They were neither of those.

They were "Human."

A Letter from Me . . .

My dearest Reader,

If I tell,

All the characters, incidents, places in this book is fictions, resemblance to any person living or dead or to any incident or place is purely coincidental, then I am not truthful. Like many of them, I was a witness of this barbarous calamity of 1999 in my loving places of Orissa and West Bengal. I heard about the protagonists from some of the victims and derived other characters and plots from my imaginary mind. After this dreaded incident on earth, whoever were victimised and lost their present, tried to construct their lives in many ways of compromising. So did Ritee and Srijesh, who not only lost their present but their invaluable future which they both have dreamt together.

For many of us, a situation comes in life where we need to choose between love and life. And whoever takes pride in choosing one above the other must realize that the joy and pain offered by both of these is almost symmetrical. Some choose life and sacrifice their love for the sake of others and when they choose love, they hurt many of them.

Like you my dear reader, I am waiting for the day when Ritee and Srijesh will choose their options. I am waiting for the day when they will meet. But I can't presume, when this auspicious moment will come for them when they choose love over life. May be when Meethi and her father will release Ritee from their house after Meethi's marriage or may be when Srijesh's mother dies and leaves her last wish for Srijesh to get settled in life. May be when Ritee feels her soul as holy and pristine to submit it to Srijesh or may be when Srijesh will justify by giving a different name to their relationship to preclude any verbal offense of our hypocritical society.

If not, may be at a time comes when Srijesh and Ritee will become old & helpless and finally decide to meet each other for the last time on the edge of death.

But I believe it will happen one day. Because . . .
They are also human too.

Your's truly
Prana Ranjan Patel

176